Family

BOOKS BY HERBERT GOLD

NOVELS • *Birth of a Hero* • *The Prospect Before Us* •
The Man Who Was Not With It • *The Optimist* •
Therefore Be Bold • *Salt* • *Fathers* •
The Great American Jackpot • *Swiftie the Magician* •
Waiting for Cordelia •
Slave Trade • *He/She* •

STORIES AND ESSAYS • *Love and Like* •
The Age of Happy Problems •*The Magic Will* •
A Walk on the West Side—California on the Brink •

MEMOIR • *My Last Two Thousand Years* •

Family *a novel in the form of a memoir*

by **Herbert Gold**

ARBOR HOUSE
New York

for Frieda Volk Frankel Gold

WHO GOES IN MUST ALSO GO OUT

1 IN AMERICA they would have a toilet for each member of the family, maybe even a day one and a night one, plus a holiday one, and a thickly shining pipe to carry the bad stuff far away from where people walked. No more throwing the bad stuff out the window. The air of America would be sweet, so sweet!

In America the children would learn to be both Jews (they already knew that in Russia) and something else—Americans!

In America people can breathe.

"What's to breathe?" the old man asked. "Now you're not breathing?"

"Air," said the old woman. "We're going."

The old man was stubborn, but the old woman was strong. She decided the family should move on to the golden Canaan. He was ready to live as much as might be allowed, and then to die right there in the fertile, humid Ukraine with his feet pointing toward Jerusalem. To the old woman this procedure seemed geographically unsound.

I call them the old man and the old woman because they were my mother's parents, but during the time of their dispute they were not yet old and I was not yet anything.

Living in the Ukraine offered the charms of wheatfields, dogs, chickens, travelers pounding through the village on horses, bargaining for eggs and leather and fur, flowers climbing against the shed in summer and snow climbing over the roof in winter. Dying in the Ukraine had the charms of cholera and murder, savage drunkenness, grief obliterated beneath further griefs, all the fault of destiny. Such living and dying was not enough for Hilda. She knew it would not be enough for the children. Perhaps she even thought far, far ahead to imagine the grandchildren for whom it was certainly not enough. She preferred blaming destiny to submitting to it; there's a difference. She stood with her hands on her hips and told her husband to look at her when she spoke to him. When he did so, she smiled because the battle was joined.

When a lady with responsibilities can locate her adversary nearby, half the battle is won. Hilda's smile had that hilarious little wiggle at the corners of the mouth which is part of the weaponry of this family's women. She looked destiny in the eyes and destiny mumbled, pulled at its chin, repeated the same old answers: he didn't want. There must be a reason.

"I want," she said. "I have more reasons than fingers."

"I have more reasons than that," said the old man, counting the hairs of his beard.

"Tell me," said Hilda. "I'm listening. Tell me your best reasons because I don't have all the time in the world."

And so, long ago, time turned inside out, when my mother was an infant, just learning to smile, her parents stared coldly into each other's eyes. Waiting to live and waiting to die had no charms for the old woman. She was impatient. The old man, who had all the time in the world, argued that God already knew where to find him; that on the day the Messiah came, he intended strolling to Jerusalem in the company of the bodies and souls of his village; that they could talk about this again next year or, God willing, the year after.

"I think we are talking about it now," Hilda said. "He must be willing."

For her what it came down to was familiar, clear, and a waste of cold stares and whispered dispute. My grandfather was satisfied where he loitered amid the smells of winter mud and summer growth, and the dust of Russia kicked in his face by Russians. My grandmother threw soapy water out the back window and made her plans. She refused to take the matter to a rabbi, especially a miracle-working rabbi, a prophesying one, because they might disagree with her. Whatever her husband decided, in his great wisdom and piety, she knew what needed to be done. The earth had tilted toward America, the village was spilling to the west, and she would not be left behind. Her husband could say whatever he wanted. Of course, since he was the head of the family, she gave him a choice—yes or no—but his *no* applied only to himself. That's freedom. That's good sense. That was her plan.

Hilda was a short plump woman who smelled of food

11

when things went well and of soap when things were difficult. Usually she smelled a little of soap and a little of cooking, which is how life is—worrisome if a person insisted on thinking that way, merely difficult if the mind was healthy. When she was young my grandmother's healthy round cheeks ran the business of her face. Later it was her watchful narrow eyes that took control, and the cheeks sank into creases, unless she blew them out, puffing and chuffing her discontent over certain household arrangements made by her own parents before her. They had obtained the agreement of God, but neglected to consult their daughter.

Without much help from the head of the family, the Frankels found their way to Cleveland, Ohio. When the ship lurched down the slope of a winter storm in the Atlantic, shattered glacial ice spinning like broken glass over the mountain-high waves, my grandfather was heartsick, my mother bumped her head, my Aunt Anna threw up, my uncles careened screaming down metal ladders, and my grandmother stared happily through the steel hull of the ship to the promised land beyond. My grandfather prayed and my grandmother cuddled her daughters. When the old man hissed at her, she said, "I'm not listening, start learning American."

A cousin from their village had already gone to Cleveland. It was the promised land of the promised land, he said. Hilda said, "We'll see about that." The old man now went where they went.

My mother's father was not a weak man; weakness had nothing to do with it; he was a scholar. With his scholar's long white and yellow beard, his scholar's bent back, his stubborn, proud, scholarly refusal to work, his holy concentration on the duty of others to care for him, his children saw him as a shadow and his wife seemed to see him as a demanding, haunting ghost. Well, he consented in advance to be pure spirit.

He was not spirit unalloyed. He was a visible invisible fact in the house. He was their only pet. *"Papa! What are you doing in there?"* He was to be cared for, and ignored in crisis. *"Papa! Stay out of there!"* Shouted at sometimes, he sulked. He kept out of the way when family business got in the way. He preferred not to be the one who was ignored, so he ignored first. He went to the synagogue. He played chess and checkers. He ate cookies. He studied not getting involved—an early practitioner of the art. Since they had come to America against his best advice, let them unriddle this place.

In this place, in America, in Cleveland, in the front yard, his wife kept a little shack of a shop, unpainted packing crates under a packing crate roof with loose nails hanging from it. She sold razor blades in case a real American passed by, wandering up Woodland Avenue; rice and sugar matted in kegs, chewing gum, brown unwrapped soap, cans of peas and peaches in yellow syrup, cans of soup, and paper packages of tea. She figured out how to grow with the century. She stood on a box behind the tooth powder and flea ointment and invited America to come to her. When the sons grew tall enough to reach doorbells, they sold light bulbs from house to house after school. They spoke American. They were ready to be unlike their father. My mother, Frieda, their little sister, preferred school to many things, but also preferred helping her mother and brothers and her big sister, Anna, who remembered the old country.

Hilda said, "In America you can prefer one thing to another, and then you can do the thing you prefer, unless you have to do the other thing."

Frieda and Anna listened with care and absorbed from their mother's words the smell of her breath, the little smile at her mouth, the decision in her eye. Then they clung to each other. They chattered in Yiddish, giggling, but the sense of their clinging was defense. They clung for shyness, but the sense of their touching was coziness and sharing. It was an intimacy in strangeness, in a bright strange world, where they were studying both poverty and money, old country and new, youth and age; if they could survive life—that was the test—they might also survive death. "The dark field gives strong bread," Hilda said to Anna, who was a stringy, harsh-haired child, already twisted and lean and shrewd, an old child as she would become an energetic and shrewd old lady. Frieda was a dumpling, blond and plump in that way of Jews who lived generations among Poles, Germans, and Ukrainians. But she did not include herself out of the dark fields which give dark bread. And she certainly did not include herself out of preferring one thing to another.

They listened to the quarrelings of Hilda and their father. "Old man!" said Hilda. "Try to pay attention."

"Are you talking to me?" he inquired.

"Old man, do I have to ask anyone else to pay attention? I want you at least sweep up a little with the broom outside."

"And now I must hurry," he said. "If I'm late, it's not good."

"Old man," she stated to the air in which the eddies of her husband left no trace. Outside, the store was unswept until Anna took the broom and Frieda took the dustrag. Hilda watched them, biting her lips.

A life without money, rich in need and God, was not what Hilda had in mind. She could not move the old man.

Anna and Frieda would learn to shake their husbands in a world of violences, riches, love and divorce, power and the abdication of power. America became more interesting when it was seized.

Hilda fought her husband over the price of a bar of soap. Frieda remembered it years later, when she fought her own husband to give up a fortune. Anna survived wrenching times, sure that everything could be made right. The children played games with matches and paper wrappers and the clotted mud of Woodland Avenue in Cleveland, where the Allegheny Mountains have their beginnings. They thought America was abstract and real, unlike Russia, which was particular and unreal. The daughters of Hilda created their world by acts of will and defiance, as men were said to do. They suffered failures of their intentions. They could be embarrassed without feeling they had sinned against nature. Women were not supposed to be so free. They surprised themselves by becoming women of this century while remaining in another. Rich soil was dark everywhere.

Hilda said to Anna, "I've got to take over. Otherwise we'll never live."

Anna said to Frieda, "Momma will do it."

Frieda decided, "So will I."

These women could not fail to make themselves the center. If this went, all went. They fought for new powers. They held the old powers together. They developed appropriate arrangements and procedures for America, for Cleveland. It was satisfactory to the old man as long as they took care of him and let him continue his chess, his checkers, and his regular prayers with his friends.

When my mother came to high school, she found she liked learning languages, social studies, history, and typing.

15

Sometimes she stayed late to help a teacher or to sit reading in the library. When Miss Reilly laughed at how she mixed up her languages, she giggled, too. She liked being corrected, so long as she didn't have to correct herself. But when Miss Reilly gave her an old pair of figure skates, she turned on the ice for hours, spinning on the steel notches, scattering slivers of ice as she scattered fragments of the language. She made up what she wanted to learn as she skimmed across the frozen rink. Her father asked in Yiddish, "Where is she? What's she hanging around? She's sixteen already, this isn't right. Let her get to work so she'll be ready to take care of her husband."

"Maybe he'll work and take care of his wife."

"Maybe so."

"When did you ever work?"

He did not deign to argue. God on high knew all he was doing. He said, "She's sixteen. Already America is spoiling her."

"You were spoiled before you were born. I haven't got time for this."

"Before I was born," he said dreamily, "I think I was a rabbi in Poland. I was a follower of the Holy One."

"You were a martyr!" his wife snapped.

He shrugged. "Maybe," he said.

"But only before you were born. Since, other people get a chance to be martyrs."

"Maybe," he added, shoulders higher than at the other maybes.

"Leave the girl alone. She's not a burden on you."

He pulled his beard and straightened it into two horns extending from his chin. "She's not as much help as she could be."

The transmigrated martyr's wife went into the front

yard of America to sell a can of yellow cling peaches and the hero of a pogrom of one or two hundred years ago, follower of one or another of the crazed holy men of Poland, unfolded his chess board. He had a clever eye when it gazed downward toward the universe of red and black squares. His task for God was to explore peace and blessedness and, today, the logic of chess—tomorrow checkers, for a little rest from thinking so far ahead. At checkers he was a champion, at chess nearly as good. He was one of the nimblest martyrs ever to fly from body to body in recent eons; a transparent pure spirit who could keep eleven moves sorted out with their alternatives behind his cupped palm over his watery blue eye atop the impenetrable depths of skull.

A little group of my grandfather's fellow former martyrs held a continual tournament in the storeroom behind the synagogue after their prayers. Sometimes also before their prayers. And even, for practice and to pass the time while waiting to argue with God about the fate of mankind, between their prayers. *Check. I take your queen.* So move. Don't think Hilda didn't know all about their prayers.

The children, however, became Americans, worked before they prayed or played, and sometimes never got around to praying or playing. In another life, if nothing else was pressing, such as bills to pay, snow to shovel, adversaries to confuse, they might find their ease and take care of the essential matters, which didn't heat the house on Woodland Avenue. But in heaven or another life, who knew what new burdens might be imposed? My mother said she could already feel my presence in her body before she was thirteen, before she even knew a man. After I went to school in the east, studied a little biology and physiology in what she came to call the Ivory League, I learned there was a kind of truth in her sensation. Something waited there for a reasonable signal to be born from her will and the erratic transmigration of a man.

Hilda told the chess-player to get out of the way of the family. Frieda and Anna twisted their hands together, but their father said nothing. The women refused consent to postponed joys, heavens at some future date, soul reborn again and again during the passing of centuries. Through their pores they absorbed the creeds of their time in America. For the synagogue chess-players and for my grandfather, the miracle truth did the little work they required of truth. It kept things steady and quiet.

Hilda, no mere greenie woman from the old country, the executive officer of a family whose gloomy and bearded head preferred prayer and chess to being an American father, took on advanced ideas and shared them with her children. She cut her conclusions into little pieces and carefully fed them, like meat, to each in turn. My mother sat near the skirts, winter rolls of skirts, and the stockings rolled down for comfort in the warm kitchen, and listened to the drone of wisdom, the pointed finger of instruction, the clacking lips and smart exhalations of breath. Knowledge came. From her mother she took things undreamed of in the neighborhood. "Shiksas can be nice, they can be beautiful," her mother muttered over the thread in her mouth.

Sometimes a quiet truth blasts a person with surprise. A person must just listen and try to understand. "Mother, you're telling me?"

"Darling, yes. It's wrong to think a shiksa will steal our men. It's wrong to think our men will run to shiksas if the blondie smiles on them."

A person must ask and try to reckon.

"Wrong, mother?"

"We are told to be charitable first of all. Didn't Akiba say we must not do unto others anything they wouldn't do unto us? The shiksa will only steal our men when we let her. So above all keep clean. Second place, our men only run to the smiling blondie with freckles all over her body if some good girl doesn't hold him back. It's not the shiksa's fault, it's the fault of our people if we keep too busy with our troubles. So let me tell you about the shiksa, darling: *she's a nice person!* She wears out young from trying too hard. She gets skinny sometimes, or maybe fat, from drinking. She works all the time, taking care of her peasant husband who beats her, because her poor children will starve otherwise."

"Mother, you work all the time."

"I got to keep the family together, don't I? You think your father could come home from shul once to keep the family together?"

Already, many years before I was conceived, Frieda felt an ache of son in her belly. "Mother," said my mother to her mother, "I don't want you to die."

"Hard work is good for me. I'm used to work. You came of good stock—no drinking except for holidays just a little bit. Look," she added, "while I'm talking, so I shouldn't waste an afternoon, you'll notice one other thing."

"You're sewing," my mother said.

"I'm sewing," her mother said. "Good girl. Smart. You'll never be a shiksa even if it was possible, God forbid, even if your hair is shiksa-colored. But thank the Lord, bless him forever—"

"Mother," my mother said.

Hilda lowered her voice to explain a secret she had discovered in the Ukraine and America. The goyim live in a world which seems as real to them as the really real world. They too seek love and to do their duty and to serve their idea of God. They too are loyal and often confused about God's will and mankind's place. They too sometimes find lazy husbands—especially those! Her heart ached for the goyim. No disrespect to her own husband, my mother's father, but his head was in the empty clouds. He came, she now understood, from a long line of shlimazls, men slipped down from the best good sense that the Lord, who was also a bit of a shlimazl, gave out in too much of a hurry. It was like a club foot or a pink eye—you can inherit it to your sons if you're not careful.

My mother started to sniffle. She suffered from nose catarrh in the humid late springtime of Woodland Avenue in Cleveland, Ohio. It came upon her especially during heart-to-heart talks with her mother.

"Drink your syrup," her mother said. "There's a remedy for everything. Or if there isn't, like the pink eye, you just live with it. Life is not, my child"—the sewing was done, she bit the thread—"life is not just what we make it. It's also how we can finagle."

My mother never forgot Hilda's wise words, her skill at cooking and sewing, her genius at keeping a family together despite the chess and checker man, her generosity toward the stranger, the goyim, and also toward the real human beings she didn't know, the Jews from elsewhere.

On this she built.

When it didn't suffice, on something else she built.

On air and intention if all else was in short supply.

Hilda said to my mother, "American girl, someday there will be the man you love. You will hold his hand and marry and have children in pain and suffering and happy or sad.

And learn no matter what you do, you will always be alone."

"Mother."

Hilda looked at her and said, "Call me mother like that. But what I said it's true anyway."

2 IN THE beginning was the thought, then the preparation, then the urgent anxiety and clatter; finally came the beach. A restful family Sunday meant screaming and hollering to get ready to holler and scream in the park. Sometimes my father actually started to back the Pontiac down the driveway without her while I fixed my eyes on the Indian brave hood sculpture and said, "You won't do it."

"I will, I will, I'm a Stalin when I get mad, I swear I will," he muttered. The worm of anger slithered in his cheek. He was trying to break the cycle of mother's running here and there, in and out, remembering vital items for the picnic baskets, switching off lights, testing the gas. She believed—so he told us—electricity would leak out through the sockets of electric lights. He knew her ways, Sam Gold *knew* her ways. When she went into Cleveland early one morning for a checkup and didn't come back till late at night, she disconnected the electric clock. Why should the hands have to turn uselessly all day like that, and maybe make a fire? Do burglars need the exact time while they're cleaning out the sterling silver?

What could a Stalin do with a wife who feared so much, poverty, bank closings, anti-Semites, electricity, gas, ruin, Father Coughlin, injury to her sons, malnutrition, the police, burglars, Negroes, Italians, Irish, beer-and-pork crazed neighbors, loose animals, bill collectors, the Depression, varicose veins, constipation, coffee nerves, and the empty-eyed men who sat on the Nickel Plate freight cars as the long trains rolled past our block? My father believed that maybe half that list deserved his personal attention, and none of it deserved constant shivering. He had the store to keep in mind, where he sold the freshest fruits on the west side. He had his idea to get out of fresh fruits and into property, which doesn't spoil overnight, as soon as he figured out what to buy it with. He had plans for empire. He didn't need her nightmare worries. What he really hated was to be kept waiting, the motor running, while his wife jiggled a faucet. "Frieda! Come on already!"

"Hold your horses, Sam. Did I pack the napkins? Do you want to eat without napkins?"

"We can use the towels, come on!"

"The *swimming* towels? Filthy! It's Sunday! You want to catch germs on Sunday? Hold your horses!"

"Frieda,"—this was his ominous Stalin voice—"we're leaving."

"But I said just a minute hold your horses," and she disappeared for the third time, running through the rear door, the screen slamming. My father backed the Pontiac out, lumping in his rage over the boulder that protected flowers from wheels. She caught us at the street, triumphant with napkins, also an extra Jell-O mold and a bottle of Mercurochrome, and we didn't get away without her.

At first my brother and I were laughing as dad zigzagged down the driveway, but it would ruin not only the day but the week if we got further than the street. She would not have forgiven the insult. Even to straighten the car in the direction of Huntington Park would have caused her to strike back. Fortunately he stopped short and she ran fast enough.

"You wasn't going without me," she stated.

"Seems like not."

She wiped her face with a swimming towel. She was the 1936 Champion of the Fifty-Foot Indoor-Outdoor Driveway Dash. "Then let's don't talk about it."

"I get aggravated when you can't get going, you keep running around the house like a chicken. That's not talking about it."

"Since we're not talking about it, I'll only say you wouldn't want to come home to a burnt-down place—a fireman stands around checking on his papers like those Irishers down the street—you would like that?"

My brother and I immediately imagined the broken bricks, the smoking fallen roof, the neighbors hanging about in secret pleasure, and therefore shouted, "We're hungry! Ice cream! Cheeseburgers!"

"Not before lunch," Mother said. "We're almost there."

We weren't almost there. We drove through Lakewood, past the car barns, through Rocky River, out past Bay Village, along the lake road where farms replaced the suburbs of Cleveland. "I like Jacksonburgers," Sid said.

"Me too. Their secret sauce and their root beer."

But we weren't getting any. We were getting home cooking on our picnic, wholesome and thought-out family food to make a strong mind for a strong body and also it would go bad if it wasn't used right away.

The Pontiac spit gravel around the parking lot. Fishermen arrived early; so did a few show-offs in two-piece bathing outfits and their girlfriends wearing heavy lipstick and tank suits and rubber hair etched into their swimcaps. Already the sun made the cocoa butter run. There was a balletic dance of kids tiptoeing with burns and blisters across the gravel. That year the fashion was not to wear slippers or shoes, if you were young and stalwart and planning to smoke your first butt before the autumn rains; in the meantime, harden the feet by struggling against earth, prickles, gravel, whatever perils the country brought. Some couples limped and necked already—stumbling with arms choking each other and toes getting wrecked by brutal pebbles. I wasn't yet ready for such madness. A tar and ammonia smell arose from the parking lot; then, beyond, green and sand and a dizzying fish whiff of Lake Erie.

"Everybody carries!" mother said—charcoal, baskets, bags, boxes. Dad took charge of the thermos and the bottles of soda. My brother Sid wondered why we couldn't just bring a few sandwiches in a bag, maybe a few bottles of pop; so did I; we were ready to learn real American eating from the real American eaters. We knew better than to express the unthinkable to our mother. *Just a couple sandwiches? You remember when your cousin Bernie almost got the rickets?*

For us, the park was a place to swim, run around, play ball with Sid's birthday hardwood hickory bat, yell and scream. For them it was a location for an outdoor meal, air and flies and sun and all that healthy contact with nature and card-players.

For us, to meet new kids.

For them, to find a game of rummy until an appetite got worked up.

For us, jumping the rolling white waves of Lake Erie.

For them, wading, cooling off, looking at the loose dogs and people, then a not-bad lunch with fruit Jell-O for dessert.

For me, to stare at the horizon—Canada straight ahead over there, the romance of foreign places where they speak Canadian.

For them, not. To look for the card-players. Maybe to unfold the Sunday *Plain Dealer* and kill the appetite reading about Hitler.

For me, to get sore at my father for paying attention only to the game of rummy.

For him, not just to play cards. For my father to win at cards, piling up the match sticks which would later be exchanged for cash. For my mother to unpack the lunch and warn my father not to lose, to consider everything, his family, the future, this being a dangerous and uncertain world; to remind him also to pay some attention to the kids so they don't grow up wild, gamblers. For my father to remark that he worked hard all week and now he was playing cards and he never lost. It's not gambling if you win. For my mother to point out that he played cards every morning at the farmer's market, while they were loading the truck with produce—how could he prove to her if he won or lost?—and he should do something else, this being Sunday, a holiday for the Americans, of which their children were now examples. For my father to say, "Be quiet,

Frieda." For my mother to say, "I'll shut up, that's what you want to tell me, but I deserve a relax, too."

"So relax," dad said. "The boys are holding a hand for me."

For family intimacy to continue amid the biting gnats and filmy mites and heat and languages and frantic dogs and thick August humidity.

Families and clans staked out picnic areas and occasional incursive tables within other areas. Sunday peace ruled; lack of war was the tradition between nationalities at Huntington Park. Italians were making spaghetti, Jews were making salads and slicing meats, some of the Irish were making whoopee. The rich brought ice chests. Puffed cheeks blew on charcoal to get things started in the WPA grates. Class distinctions made little difference among fire-starters, though there were isolated instances of kerosene. For a while mother, in her black cotton bathing dress with the modest flap of skirt, came down to the beach to watch my brother and me bobbing on the whitecaps of Lake Erie. She wrinkled her nose. "What kind of smell is that? What kind of fish?"

"Inner tube," I said.

She checked invisible Canada out there. She checked the sky for cloud or storm. She had asked a lifeguard and, although he was a goy, believed him—no sharks in Lake Erie. She warned us not to drown or let a dog bite us or pick fights with strangers. "You could catch an affection," she whispered. She waded. She said, "Oooh, ooh, it's so cold, it's nice, it's warm, don't let your lips turn blue."

Her spirit took a relax in the peace of the Christian sabbath. We would keep an eye on each other, she decided, we had friends, we would take care not to walk out toward Canada where the water got deep and there might be sharks after all (how could you prove the *lack* of something? from not being bit by even one?); we had learned to swim, we used the buddy system, we were junior lifesavers. A careful review of all the facts allowed her to go back to fix lunch. Now there was a subject which deeply engaged her. We promised to come up from the beach when the noon whistle blew.

The noon whistle blew. The beach dogs yapped and yipped at the high-pitched sound; one of them extended its throat like a wolf and howled. Regretfully we left the sand spit, my brother and I. We could imagine potato salad and sliced tomatoes and tunafish, also cold pot roast with horse radish and pickles, and for once our mother seemed to have some good ideas. Swimming, jumping waves, and making contact with new close friends and their Goodyear inner tubes were a few of the basic causes of appetite. I promised a wiry Protestant to return to the beach in half an hour. Sid asked a responsible Catholic to guard the sand city they were building together and to keep the animals from running through it, especially that nervous dog over there, which was making shrill squeals and running in circles, chewed by fleas or maybe just overheated. My brother wanted to bet with me—the fruit Jell-O would be melted. "What's melt?" I asked him. "How soft is melt?"

In some ways I took after my father and mother, ever questioning. The parochial school boy, Timmy his name was, only answered questions.

Sid waved to the Catholic and he waved back. The gravity-defying dog was lurching sideways up the hill through the wild asparagus, snapping at tufts of grass and making hurt undog voices, like a person imitating a mongrel. Maybe it had reason to believe it was a person.

We climbed the slats from the beach to the picnic area

28

above. Lake sand gave way to mixed sand and dirt into which trees and shrubs had sunk roots. It was gradual and mysterious, like how children change into people who are allowed to eat whatever they want, grass into asparagus, good nature into other. From the farms nearby, asparagus seeds had blown, and taken hold, and spiky straggles clung to the edges of the shore. These energies of the vegetable world interested my brother and me. The yipping dog interested us both as it ran in little circles, and yet moved through these circles up the slope, making wasteful progress, sending sandspins and avalanche lumps down toward the lake. It didn't seem to have enough good sense to use the slats on which barefoot kids climbed, getting slivers in their toes and soles, toughening up for the end of the summer. The dog whirled upward against gravity, emitting that odd high-pitched gargling squeal.

Our picnic table was piled with goodies. Dressings of raisins—no, sunkissed flies—picked and chose. The air was filled with mites. My brother's baseball bat lay across the napkins. "Oh-ho, have I got something good for you," mother said, as if we didn't know. "Call your father first. He don't come when I call him."

It was my job, as the elder, to claim him away from the card-players. I didn't like this job, although he only held his grudge until something else came up. Something else always came up. But his scowl was enough to darken the sky. Interruption did not please him. When a loser, he was peeved; a winner, irked; no way for me to come out ahead in this job. I struggled to break even with my father. "Dad," I said, "time for lunch."

"Is your bathing suit wet?"

"Everyone's waiting."

"You can't eat with a wet bathing suit."

"Dad."

"They can wait five minutes. You see I'm busy don't you? I'm finishing the hand."

I hung nearby a moment. One of his friends winked at me. There would be no further communication from the author of my being, not at this moment in the perilous history of rummy. I limped on my bruised toe back to mother. "About a half hour," I said.

The dog which had yelped and followed us, spinning sideways up the slope, suddenly speeded its endeavors. It was howling and snapping at invisible enemies. It was a ginger animal with the face of an alligator—a sharp and blunt alligator's snout—soapy foam at its lipless mouth. My brother looked frightened and pulled closer to me. I pulled closer to him. Mother was thinking out loud, "Sex crimes I thought they commit in parks, that's why we pay our taxes—"

I tried to understand her.

"For the police. But this stuff besides the stuff you wouldn't even know—the dogs also bite persons when they're not even hungry—"

And someone screamed. The dog had nipped a baby on its blanket, raking the flesh and tearing off its bootie. The shriek came from a parent; the child's mouth was open; it had not yet discovered its pain. Something new was detonated in the animal by the taste of pink bootie threads, ropy droplets of blood, and now suddenly it seemed to be biting in all directions as a howling and crying arose from the flutter of Sunday newspapers, the spill of food, the splattering charcoal fires. The dog was snapping the air and what was in the air. The dog was not biting to eat. The dog was simply biting. The dog was mad.

Fur and spit hurled among the picnickers. Bottles and

paper cups tumbled. Spaghetti like white worms suddenly crawled in an immense heap on the beaten ground. A loose puddle of thick tomato blood dripped from a bench. A mother screamed without words and a father screamed instructions. From far away, when I looked at my own father, I seemed to catch a puzzled glance at the commotion as he raised a winning card in his slapping slamming gesture. The dog made torture noises, barks, snarls, broadcasts from a central office of destruction. I smelled something like what my father put on his face after shaving. The mad dog was almost a familiar enemy. I wished my Catholic new friend had come up from the beach to see. The dog made abrupt squeals and darts and its eyes were red and blank.

Terror switched everything around. The faces of the kids in the park, suddenly deprived by fear of their childhood, looked like ancient agonized adults. The faces of the grownups, helpless with fear, deprived of their maturity, suddenly became thin and skeletal and childlike as they shouted and ran and tried to hide babies behind their bodies. In Europe, dive bombers were aloft, and Hitler came to kill. Here we were lucky, and yet even here on Sunday a mad dog was loose. I stood without moving, the moment printing itself on me, until my mother jerked me around, seizing my arm, and I stumbled; and then as I skidded alongside the path where the dog headed into me, my mother fell forward toward the animal, which seemed up close the size of a wolf, a horse, a gorilla, spewing noise and saliva and clots of mud and perhaps skin from those it had bitten—she fell on it. I could feel its panting heat like a piece of machinery near my neck.

My mother fell on the dog with the bat in her hands, and bounced away from it. As she pulled off I saw that the dog's head had been smashed, a crumple of brains leaking inside, the blood-spotted eyeball hanging by a cord, staring at me; the grinding of half a dog's head continued, a death thrash from somewhere deep in nature; and the bat came up again and again—I didn't see my mother's bat come down—the dog being broken into earth in a shape of fur and teeth and muck.

The screams continued. A haggard circle gathered about the destroyed animal, bloody meat and bones and eyeball hanging by a string of flesh into the distressed brain. The body heaved and twitched as if it still needed to bite. It steamed with some mortal internal cookery. This was also nature. A park policeman in a green twill jacket gave orders: "Stand back, stand back now. This could be dangerous."

Someone began to curse him in Italian.

"All right, you. You're in this country now. Cleveland ain't Naples—we don't use that ilk of language here. I may have to report you to the county officer."

The curses rolled on and the park policeman said, "I'm doing this Sunday crowd handling best I can without any help. Stand back. Stand back, you people."

Mother leaned slack and wet against a tree. The policeman said, "Give this Jewish lady some air, people."

The ambulances rolled and bumped across the green. The children—why was it only children?—who had been bit were strapped onto gurneys. One mother insisted on holding her child; both of them were crying.

My father said, "Frieda, that was *schoen* what you did."

"You wasn't here. You was playing cards."

"I didn't see. You handled it good."

"Mother," I said.

"Easy," she said. "When you got to live with anti-Semites, everything else is easy."

"What does that have to do with it?" I asked.

"My bat is all dirty," my brother said. "I need a new hardwood hickory."

"You'll get it," my father said. "Frieda. Frieda." I think this was the first time I saw him simply put his arms around her. You want to go home now? Maybe we left the screen door unlocked."

"Wait a minute. No jokes. Tired."

She bent out of his grasp and reached for my shoulder, as if she needed help to lie down. But resting wasn't her business. Mother, this crazed protector, this heavy lady leaning against a tree, slid toward the ground and kneeled, holding my chin in her fingers like a flirtatious woman. She stopped running history through her mind and took my head in her hands. "If I had a girl," she said, "I suppose I wish I did, but I'm not sure she'd be pretty."

Did she want me to argue? To insist I'd be pretty if I were a girl? I wouldn't do that.

She kissed me on the lips. I had never received such a kiss, not that I could remember. "Your father got me, he don't need a girl. And I got you. And we sure had a picnic today."

She did not want me dying in her lifetime; I would have to die in my own. "Can I go say goodbye to a nice Catholic?" I asked. "He's watching our stuff. Can I tell him how I almost got bit?"

"Don't go. Stay here with me."

My father went to huddle behind a tree with his friends. They were settling up, matches for money. He returned smiling. He had won nearly forty dollars. He was sorry to miss the dog, but a man can't be everywhere at once. Fortunately he had a helper, but he was also puzzled. "She can do a thing like that, grab a kid's bat, take care of that hound when all these big strong Eyetalians was only yelling. So why can't she make a picnic without it's got sand in the potato salad?"

She held my chin and drew me closer for inspection. "No," she said. "You'll fight. I don't know if you'll win."

Again she was not answering my father, not listening to me. But she was thinking. I smelled the slaughtered beast in the air, and very soon I took to reading the newspapers to try to find out what such things mean, what my mother meant.

3 MOTHER'S PALE eyebrows furrowed together because I brought Tom Moss home every day after school for oatmeal cookies, not that she didn't want him to enjoy the cookie which is a meal in itself, raisins, nuts in season, her special formula, once a coconut, maybe a sesame seed, who knows, a chopped fig, sometimes good ingredients wild Cossack horses themselves couldn't drag out the secret, plus a couple glasses of milk to wash it down and introduce calcium into the boys' plumbing, all the best elements for American nutrition. But Tom came to my house and I didn't go to his. She understood why. His mother used to allow me in when I was five or six and we first became best friends. As adolescence approached, she began to worry about the future bad influences, the funny business starting, imperative Jewish glands spurting.

What a pleasure later that I could learn to be *bad*, talk with hands, be bad and outrageous, make noise, breathe on people! What freedom, what fun! Like a Negro! But in the meantime, when I walked with Tom, I stopped at his front sidewalk and we spoke fluent Lutheran to each other: *Uh. See ya.*

It tended to cause a fellow to turn inward. In Lakewood, in the middle thirties, as the Depression was beginning to end in the preparation for war, I headed for my house alone, passing the black housemaids heading for the streetcar. I wondered if there were so many black women, why weren't there any black men?

Later, of course, in higher education and in adult life, this was reversed. Black men were in plentiful supply, but black women disappeared. "My son goes to collitch to the Ivory League, Columbia," my mother stated, "he says it's the gem of the ocean. Western Reserve is good enough for everybody, all the best doctors, lawyers, but not him. Lots of fine specialists come from Western Reserve, ear men, nose men, throat men, allergies, psychologists, they all come out of Western Reserve highly recommended if they can get in, but him, my boy, no—he thinks he's too liberal arts for Cleveland. Now he struggles, of course. How can he make a living? Even his friend Tom, the anti-Semite's boy, will make a better living."

The gems of the ocean didn't help a boy set up a nice little practice.

It helped a little to know what I was eating, good ingredients, and she hadn't minded feeding Tom Moss. She fed the cousins who attended Western Reserve and Columbus. She fed the ones who went for specialist and those who decided it was okay to be a glass man, also—glaziers. She fed the time-payment cousin who kept changing jobs, furniture, jeweler, automotive. Sales can be a profession, too. Sales got to eat just like anybody else. She fed the nurses and the teachers. She sent out the posse for cousins to feed on national holidays; religious holidays, it went without saying. And she fed the stricken seekers of the thirties as they shambled down our street, looking to rake leaves or shovel snow or do a job of cement patching. If only everyone gave everyone else a little sandwich, a little something hot, how much friendlier, how much sturdier the whole world would all be!

Now there were things about my life she couldn't control. Still, she needed to know I had a girlfriend; I needed to let her know. At age nineteen, a year in the Army already, it seemed more important to pass the thrilling secret to my mother than it was to sneak the same victory to my fellow soldiers in the day room, the shower room, on the firing range at Fort Bragg. The 100th Infantry Division was preparing to fight its way into Germany. This wasn't enough for me. I needed adult life, besides.

"Is she Jewish?" my mother asked hopelessly, as she always did—*How many killed? How many Jews?*

I felt the little smile fighting out of my evil heart. "Yes," I said.

"Finally in the end!" she cried. "You're growing up! So when you getting married?"

I was shaking my head, negative, negative; and laughter was following upon the evil smile, choking me with the old reliable pleasure of upsetting my mother.

"A barman keeps hard hours, I know that, but she can go

to sleep early, do her hair, help out sometimes, okay a soldier boy doesn't need help in his business, but do you think this war is going to last forever?"

I had told her I was a barman. She didn't know this referred to the Browning Automatic Rifle, although she wondered if I used a sunlamp to get so brown, played a lot of football to get so rough. She thought I had been appointed to serve the officers nice cool drinks when they came in from a hard day's warfare. I wanted to twist her, but not to worry her, so I let her tell her sister barman, let Aunt Anna warn her not to permit drinking habits—not this son!

I was on a furlough home in Cleveland, Ohio, thinking about Fayetteville, North Carolina, where life and death, love and pride and maybe a touch of revenge were being played out in various games of war and trials of lust. France was our likely next stop.

This was my last night in Cleveland. Tomorrow I would take the Greyhound bus back to my real home, the Army. I sat at the kitchen table with a bowl of Wheaties, mother's stewed prunes, mother's canned peaches, mother's advice and counsel. This was not only the Breakfast of Champions, but also the late night snack of heroes before they go forward to breathe Greyhound diesel and barman's lignite and powder.

My father passed back and forth through the thick slam of the screen door. He looked in on my sleeping younger brothers. My mother and I needed a little talk, and that was okay with him, but he had a little nervous pacing to accomplish before he was ready for sleep. He stood at the window, in the way he had, considering the world by counting the stars. The war worried him, the future worried him, security worried him. The past did not concern him, our kitchen talk did not interest him. In the sky there were more stars than anyone knew.

My mother's excitement was flaming. She was in a rush for a daughter-in-law, since she had never had a daughter; she longed for grandchildren, since that came next on her schedule.

"I'll visit to Fagleberg, I won't get in your way, I promise, maybe a little ginger ale in a dark corner, just the three of us, you know me, just a little peek at your future wife—"

Fayetteville was a town of enlisted men's wives doing laundry, a few distraught mothers being proud and brave and bored, officers with epaulets and MPs strolling in pairs, looking for men with sleeves rolled up or hats not on heads or drunk or AWOL. An exhausted southern town, wooden houses leaning crazily, sinking into red sand; and the nervous leaky spending of an Army base. She wanted to find the lounge where I served as barman, but I told her it was forbidden. The range where I fired .50-caliber clips into the dunes and lost some of the hearing of an ear was off-limits to mothers. And also the lady of my life at this moment was not for presenting to my mother.

"Mother," I said, "you're going too fast."

"You said she's a nice girl—thanks God!"

"Mother, she's married."

My mother had developed the skill of cramming a great deal of silence into a few seconds. The moment was thick with rue, shock, meditation, and rapid recovery. Decision processes were engaged. The world demanded action. Her lips parted, saying, "She's," and closed again. Fury, grief, and mastery of herself ensued. "She's," she said. "Are you joking again? Why do you always have to torture and joke?"

"No."

"What's her name?"

"Michelle Malkin."

"Married or single?"

"That's her married name. Maiden name Epstein, Michelle, no-middle-initial. He's a dentist."

"The husband?"

"Yes."

"So that's nice for her at least, that's good, that's sensible." She was estimating fast. "A girl goes and marries a dentist, she got a head on her shoulders." She was still figuring. The decision gears had tendencies and reverses I didn't suspect. "Leaves him for you, but, she's a dummy. What's his family going to say? Don't he have a mother, father, they'll go crazy?"

"Ma," I said. "She hasn't left him."

She put her head in her hands. She whispered, "A dull tree?"

I nodded.

"In wartime?"

I nodded.

"You're a morale-breaker?"

"I know," I said, "but he doesn't. So you see Jewish isn't everything."

My mother believed that sometimes a person has to think of several factors at once. In her view, life shouldn't be like that, but God never asked her view. Even some of the Holy Commandments contradicted each other—what if the neighbor you loved was someone's wife? It was supposed to be clear, but it wasn't. "What kind of dentist?" she asked. "Root canal and gums or straight?"

"I never asked, ma. He's on the post now. They live in Officers' Housing."

"Can't they shoot you for doing that dull tree meshugga

stuff to an officer? He finds out, it could interfere with the fillings."

"They can't shoot me for it. I suppose the dentist could, but nobody else is supposed to."

"Why are they so white?" She was looking at her knuckles, not my teeth. "Because I want to personally kill you a few questions is why. Okay, okay, let me think. You serious about this dull tree woman?"

I took a bite of graham cracker, a sip of milk, and said, "She's the most wonderful person in the world."

She winced, but made an effort. "Watch your tongue," she said. "Remember I'm your only mother, you should have no other before me. Irregardless, if you're telling nothing but the truth and the whole truth, we got some thinking caps to shoot off. I suppose her husband hits her? Runs out on her? He's cruel and unusual? He's one big mistake-and-a-half?"

"I don't know," I said. "She never mentioned."

"She don't love him, he's so disgusting? A pig around the house? Doesn't clean up after himself?"

"Maybe," I said. "Could be. Don't know."

Her eyes narrowed and the yellow flecks seemed compressed by emotion. "Don't make me mad now. You got to give a help. I'll try, but you got to do your part, son. Nothing in this life comes easy, even your having fun with the drunk dentist's—he runs out on her—wife."

She pushed the box of graham crackers across the enameled kitchen table, closer to me, handier like that, poured milk into my glass—*thanks God the barman isn't a shicker* —and began a story that, with all her lifelong conversation, she had never found the time to tell. When she spoke, she liked to use breath but not waste the air. Now there came

41

an emergency in her life which required the exercise of history.

The Story of the Pharmacist

Once upon a time my father was not my mother's first man. Later he became the first and only man in her life, but it didn't begin that way. He was not my mother's starter husband. Before romance began, a pharmacist hung about the family, talking of pills and jars and hoods who read the magazines standing up, sneaked penny candies, smudged *True Detective* with licorice and chocolate, so that the real customers said, "Yech! A used bookstore you run here?" One kid went so far with criminal chutzpah as to put his finger all the way behind the counter into the ice cream, the chocolate ice cream—the pharmacist gave him a whack, plus charged him a nickel, which he paid upon the threat of a little talk with his parents. Well, he didn't pay it, didn't have it in any of his pockets, but he promised to bring it next time.

Even as a girl, my mother had observed, "Won't going-a be no next time."

"Smart girl smart," said the pharmacist, gazing at her with a lovelight flaring up behind the thick glasses of a reliable professional man, and at once began negotiations with my grandmother, my mother's brothers and sisters, and even a little, out of innate courtesy, with the float-haired greenie who happened to come along as my grandfather. The pharmacist sought the smart-girl-smart's hand in marriage.

Granted, was the consensus.

42

Granted, was my grandmother Hilda's verdict.

My mother thought of the boy with the chocolate ice cream finger and laughed. When the pharmacist with a nice pharmacy right on a nice corner of Woodland Avenue asked why, this was serious, she said, "Chocolate ice cream finger," and giggled some more.

Her older sister Anna said, "Pay attention. It's about how you're going to be a woman."

"Enough," said my grandmother. *Genugb.*

The pharmacist was ten years older, maybe more, uglier, maybe really not a good looker, fatter, would get even fatter, and heavier in the head and spirit than he ought to be for an ice skating youngest daughter of a prominent Woodland Avenue greenhorn family. But on the other hand my mother saw no reason not to accept his invitation. The pharmacist wore sharp little black pointy shoes; he carried a sharp little pointy white belly under the knit undershirt (she peeked once, never mind how). He had a nice little pharmacy, a drugstore, at the streetcar stop on the corner two corners away—she could visit her real family daily. The streetcar ran down Woodland and St. Clair; it ran everywhere in Cleveland and the known America in those days. She would be secure with a pharmacist. There would be wholesale powders and potions; come heck or high water, there would always be ice cream. She sat by herself for ten minutes and folded her hands in her lap like the girl on a swing in a calendar she liked. She considered the matter. She said: *I guess so.*

You mean it? he asked, drenched with reciprocated love. She could still go ice skating sometimes if she liked that sort of Yankee thing. He understood how a girl might need fun, even foolish Yankee fun, not get serious just yet even if she has the good luck to marry a truly serious person. At sixteen, maybe she could still take a little skate now and then. He would mind the store and gradually she would learn to mind him. He was patient. He promised that, too. Men promise anything when they're drenched with desire.

My grandfather mumbled through his yellow and white beard that she was just a baby and ought to go to work for her own family first. But she was no baby. She would be nearly nineteen in two years.

The pharmacist shot nervous love smiles at her. She had sort of said yes, looking at her mother, Hilda, not at him. The sort of yes seemed to be a sort of assent to the duties of a drugstore wife. The pharmacist honored an expression of submission to long hours. When he smiled, she noticed a construction site of ruined teeth. She decided to do what she had planned to do, promised to do, but hoped he wouldn't smile too much once they were married. . . .

While my mother told her story, in the next room my father switched on the radio for the late night news of the war. I was listening to the news of my mother. She leaned and whispered to me over a bowl of Wheaties and a package of graham crackers in Cleveland, Ohio, in the midst of a disaster of history and my pleasure with the dentist's lady: "Tried to kiss me with that awful mouth open! And I wasn't yet sixteen years old even, a baby."

She had just said she was nearly eighteen, or was it nineteen—my mother's mathematics always presented difficulties—and I noted how the elastic quality of my age, depending on what she wanted to claim as my duty or deny as my right, applied retroactively to herself. It drew me to her. We were dealing with kin here.

"Just seventeen, hardly more than sixteen years old, let's skip the whole wedding, quite a few nice presents, those are only details, so then I was living in an upstairs rental unit, cooking for this pharmacist—okay, that's only right, he was my provider—but not so refined as he gave out to my family, plus he ate and kissed with his mouth open. Little things like that start to matter. You call such a thing a marriage?"

"Mother," I said, my hands sweating around my garrison cap. In the distant past of that last evening at home, I must have intended to walk around the block with my father.

"You just said *mother*, are you asking? Wait. First a point I got to say, plus now you know. The deal is: it's important for your future."

My future, if she could only stop hatching family for me, was to shoot a heavy repeating weapon, the Browning Automatic Rifle, and lose a little hearing but not my life. My future was to enjoy the dentist's wife because I could hear her whisperings despite the ringing in my right ear, and because this whispering seemed to give me no choice in the matter—not when what I wanted so much was to enjoy the lady and she, for whatever her antidental reasons, was meeting me nine-tenths of the way and summoning me with her wet lips the rest of the one-tenth. I was a soldier boy and she was an older woman. My present and future plans had been to let life take me.

Now my future was to remember forever after how my mother had taken a husband before my father, who was still indifferently frowning over the news out of our Zenith.

"So the pharmacist gets jealous," she was saying. "Not enough for him to run a nice little corner drugstore, he wants me I should help out in the store, keep an eye on me, but I think better I learn to take care of the house, cook a healthy full course meal, get ready maybe for a kid if I can stand the teeth. But no, he falls in love, a funny kind of love is such a love, he wants I should also be a clerk, wait on trade. He thinks I'm meeting somebody all day long. Secrets, he thinks. He wants to lock me in. He wants to tie me down with balls and chains. He wants I should do nothing but wait for him—*who was that, who was I talking on the phone?* My mother I was talking on the phone! My brothers, my sister Anna, doesn't a good person talk to family on the phone? So I give him secrets. I make my plans."

A glint of angry pleasure came into the yellow-flecked eyes. She liked remembering any successful plan, and particularly this one. It was get-away time as she lowered her voice and held my hand across the table—not so tightly, of course, that I couldn't use it to reach for food if appetite flared up.

"So one day he was stacking the magazines, I suppose, the day they were delivered, like he always did, *Liberty*, the *Saturday Evening Post*, *Reader's Digest*, all the magazines, he counted to make sure the jobber brought him the right number, they tend to rook a little. He was stacking, I was packing. Upstairs in the unit I put in boxes, just threw things in. The clothes, the wedding stuff, only what was mine, my side's stuff. The truck came. My brother. Wowee! Vroom! I jumped in. I was home again. No more Mister-Stupid-Pharmacist-with-the-Magazines. If I saw him again, I don't remember."

"Did you ever talk with him again?"

"I don't remember."

"Ever see him?"

"Don't remember. Or if I do, that's mine to know and yours not to know. So far I go, but no farther."

"Will you tell me later?"

"I told you now, didn't I? I tell you what's good for you. Tear my tongue out, that's enough for today."

"Okay," I said.

But ideas have significance, and significance was stirring in her. "The rest, if there is anymore, God only knows, I'll tell you what you deserve if you ever need. Right now you need a little bit. Bless you and marry this nice Jewish girl who first should get a divorce in her home state from some jealous nervous person, probably drinks, I don't care if he's a professional, what's a tooth man? Does he take laughing gas? Someday, when this war is over, knock on wood, you'll also get to be a professional, even if temporary you're a barman—he doesn't need her, a man who had to go for dental because he couldn't make medical, like you need her. Those days then—"

She thought she saw consternation on the PFC barman's face, and she thought she knew why. "Those days then," she said, whispering the really dirty part, "what I needed for a husband was your father."

It was a lot to learn on furlough from the 100th Infantry Division at Fort Bragg on a Sunday evening of the war. I learned some new parts about life, and there was much I did not know. I had never mixed or shaken a drink but I could name the parts of the Browning Automatic Rifle; this was correct. Soon many of my fellow barmen would be dead. My mother came to focus on finding the proper wife and not turning the lady away because a mere filler of teeth stood between us. The Nazis, she promised heaven, were doing worse things than I was doing. Of course, the Nazis might not be forgiven. With her own history she testified to the fact that the commandment about avoiding thy neighbor's wife does not apply in cases of extreme urgency, such as the first Jewish girl of a deprived existence. Furthermore, she offered herself, wife and mother, as living and breathing heavily proof of the virtue of divorce. Since marriage is a sacrament, some people even say it's holy, is it not profaned and a stench in God's eyes when a girl stays married if unhappy? In that case she wouldn't have been free to marry my father and I might be stacking magazines or helping out with pills at this very moment. In fact, I would be somebody else altogether—how would I like that?

I wouldn't like being somebody else, a puffy junior druggist. I preferred being the son of my gambling father, a good provider with a heart full of secrets.

In my mother I began to see a glimmer of reason, or even better, of unreason; but there was more. I tasted graham in my mouth; I longed for the taste of the older woman, the wife in Fayetteville.

"Since personally I don't acquaint with the lady," my mother admitted, "naturally I can't give advice and I'm not doing so. But if a *dentist* thought she was okay, she'll pass for a professional, she must got a head or two on her shoulders. Plus she's willing to take a chance on you—a head on her shoulders plus smart plus she loves you, dummy, plus the right background. A ketch."

"A catch," I muttered, romance dribbling away in my mother's tide of approval.

"So I said," she remarked primly. "Like I personally was a ketch when your father found me, not spoiled goods or merchandise, am I?"

"You're a catch, ma."

She glared. She did not understand how the issue of her body could still speak differently, wrongly; have secrets differently, wrongly. Despite what people say, there are no mirrors, or mirrors lie—anyway, was I a stranger? Hadn't she done everything to bring us close, including bearing me in her belly for nine months, longer if necessary, and then as a worse burden for nineteen years? "This lady of yours," she said, "go and do likewise. I'm asking very sincerely, son, show me the girl. I'll come to Fagleberg. And about her divorce—" She was whispering again. "Mum's the word. I'll just tell family, Anna."

Family and Aunt Anna included most of the east side of Cleveland. The lady would not be leaving the dentist for me, she might not leave him at all, I would pine only for a season, the war would continue, and nothing in love or anything else was settled for me or anyone but my mother. For her things were continually being resettled. Mum would be the word here, too. Mum required many family consultations.

But I learned something even if I didn't settle the matter. The romance of my parents was not only a valentine story, a meeting at the City Ice & Fuel Skating Rink, love at first glide, hot chocolate with marshmallows, slipping into each other's lives with no impediment but the sons to come. Love had another concerned party. At the edge of the valentine stood the pharmacist, weeping and shaking with shame and jealousy.

"He hung around on the street in front of our rental, so dad went out and showed him his fruit hammer," my mother said. "Under his nose your father showed it. He carried on. He cried. I told him to find himself another girl, a nice girl who likes clerking. He went back to the store and put some tablets—you know, pills? dummy ones?—in his mouth and they found him on the pile of magazines. If that's love, son, try to be sensible."

The next morning I was heading back toward Simulated Attack on the red sands of North Carolina. Eventually I would try with mixed success, no different from the pharmacist who almost became my father, to be kind, sensible, and loving. But first I had to learn to kill.

"Dumb letter he wrote to me," she was saying. "You think I kept that letter? Tore it in a million pieces, burned it, flushed it. He was the man first made me a woman. No sense in those dumb words. Aggravated me for years with that letter, and you were right here in my belly already, and me crying and crying. Don't you ever think dumb words are going to get your way for you, son."

There were tears in her eyes and she was smiling. "Give what's right. Take what's right. If you don't love, don't love; but if you love, love."

4 WE WERE brought out of barracks to stand at attention when President Roosevelt died. When a new bomb was dropped over Japan, and then another, we were told we might not have to join forces with the Russians in Japan after all. We were being thrust suddenly out of the years of following orders, boredom, and death. I had entered the Army near my eighteenth birthday. Now I was twenty-one. I had grown accustomed to this childish concentration on warfare. Some of us were not ready to leave our uniforms and take up adult life, which like death, no matter how close, seemed at that age to be merely an ominous rumor.

51

In April 1946 I loafed about home on terminal leave. I had my orders. They gave me an interval here. I wasn't sure what to do with unassigned time except to read an endless book by Marcel Proust and fill out papers for starting back to school. I felt obscurely bereft, having to decide the rest of my life. My awed brothers, even my mother and father, tried not to interrupt whatever they thought I was doing with myself. I was relieved, happy, lonely, and distraught. Something was over—my life as a soldier, with a soldier's freedom—and I had no good idea of what should replace it.

One afternoon when I was out for a beer with Tom Moss, exchanging three years of war stories, my mother took my GI paratroop boots to Goodwill, she gave away my fatigues, she informed me the Army was finished. On the campus at Western Reserve they wear a business suit and a briefcase, she told me. I told her I was absolutely going away to Columbia College. She didn't give up.

"What's so ninety-nine and forty-four percent pure about the Ivory League?" she asked. "It floats more than Western Reserve? You get to be a cleaner professional in Columbia than right here at home where all the good eye men, nose men, throat men come for the best training *plus.*"

"I'm not even going to be a doctor, mother."

"Plus home cooking. Anyway, how do you know what kind of doctor you're going to be? Don't try to be a prophet, also. A little humble, please, for the person who happened to suffer more than anybody to give birth to a boy with a big head like you—some respect, if you please. Maybe, okay, you don't want hard hours, you'll be an allergy or a real estate man—not that's so bad, neither."

Her words rippled and flowed, rushed and twisted in eddies, reminding me of her intentions for the future and the past, ceaselessly advising, letting out the terror (it was undiminished), emitting calmness (it was unattainable), asking surcease of sorrow and humbly demanding total capitulation. I resisted. I had a big head. I dug in.

As her eldest son, I had been nursed too well with a stubbornness like her own. But when truly vengeful and determined, I fell silent—then what could she say? How to say shut up to a person with lips pressed together?

"Answer. Why not Western Reserve College?"

"I'd like to go to New York." This was my Paris, my London town, my Manhattan, my intention to find a way out of Cleveland, Ohio.

"Nothing much there," she said. "No family in New York, only a few cousins."

I shrugged.

"Dirty you wouldn't believe. Noisy likewise. A nice clean Forest City you got here in our city of Cleveland."

Shrugged again.

"You see? You can't even answer with a good discussion."

Silence.

"So be quiet then. When the patients tell you sore throat, cough, catarrh, you're looking at them like that and give not a word for their money? Even a real estate man got to comment sometimes, diagnose a leaky roof, a furnace."

I went to New York. I met a girl who was clever, delicate, pretty, and willing to abide with me in a basement off Amsterdam Avenue where all we could see was the shoes and ankles of the passersby, the slush in winter and the blowing grime in summer. Naturally, although it hadn't occurred to me in advance, since we were living together and would quarrel, we would make up after the quarrels;

and one of the ways to make up a quarrel between an unmarried couple is to marry. We married.

We had two children, which are permanent. We had what seemed to be some happy times, which ended. When you win through to kindness in the troubles of marriage, the troubles become elements of sumptuous achievement, part of the happiness. When in the end you lose, each trouble is a premonition which should have provided clear warning, a demand to change course before it was too late.

The lady and I thought we wanted to be happy together, and summed up the world in each other. The marriage crashed.

A general rule about trouble in marriage applies to most retiring husbands: makes the stomach smaller inside; and trouble often shrinks the outside, too. In my case, I got skinny. This shrinking and shriveling has little to do with eating. I was reduced by feeling small. Complex diminishment procedures were taking place. I contracted. To sum up for perfect clarity: going narrow and nervous and somewhat null.

I was fresh out of oceanic feelings of belonging to the entire universe. Looking at myself through the wrong end of the telescope, my body accepted the evaluation of others and took to retraction. Like a boy, not like a husband and father. Like a child.

"Oh, no," said my mother when I came to visit in Cleveland in the summer of 1956. "Not only you lose a wife, but you lose weight, also. What's the matter with you?"

"I can get that back," I said. "I don't think I'll get the wife back."

"What do you want for dinner?"

"I ate on the plane."

"How many times I tell you never never never eat on the

plane, that rotten plane food, the altitude makes it go bad, you're coming home lunchtime or dinnertime? The height ruins the cooking. You think those stewardesses know how to bake a decent popover? So instead, since you pay for it with the ticket anyway, you can maybe take a sandwich to go."

"They don't give sandwiches to go, ma."

She fell silent. She brooded upon the unfeeling routine of paying for airline food, it's the rules, and yet a person can't reserve his appetite for dinner at home with his family but pack up a nice little sandwich to go for later, a snack, an emergency feeding. She didn't appreciate waste. Still, if they serve a lunch or a dinner, okay, that's the way things are. There's no justice in the feeding habits of America. You can't fight United Airlines. However, there is a remedy. She noted with grief for my situation, averting her eyes, "So eat twice. Wouldn't hurt. Sin and bones."

"You mean skin," I said.

"Why you leave your wife?" she demanded. "I read where Ike almost divorced Mamie, he had this girl driver driving for him, it was wartime, people get crazy, but then again he didn't. So even if I never liked the stuckup little lady you had to pick out from typical dumb stubbornness you inherited out of your father, she was cute. I'll give her that. Cute. *Cute*, but not one inch more. So why you do a thing like that?"

"Ma," I said.

"From all the nice persons you could have asked, that lovely dentist's wife you told me about, a veteran like you were, GI Bill, smart, good family—you could asked me an advice, I'd tell you what I feel in my heart—and then after you went and did it anyway, to compound the story, now a *divorce?*"

"Ma," I said, "you left your first husband—"

"Sha! A little respect!"

But she knew I would fight back. I must have inherited that bad habit from someone else in the family. "—you left your husband when nobody did that, ma."

A tight little smile commanded silence. Silence and crossed arms commanded more silence. During this stasis, as a climax to reproach, empty air heaped upon throbbing empty air, she interrupted herself with words. "What you just said is irreverent."

"Irrelevant, ma."

"A boy with two baby kids divorces his wife doesn't get to correct my English. That was a whole different story. I was smart. Poor greenies on Woodland Avenue, naturally I made a mistake. But right away I saw who the ball bounces, plus no kids. Plus I'll tell you the story since you're kind enough to ask." She paused to defy me not to ask. I didn't not ask. "All right. He was a jealous druggist tried to tell me all the time pharmacy, pharmacy—why should a girl like me stay with such a person? You trying to tell me your cute little wife I never liked but that's a besides the point was a jealous druggist? Is that what you're telling? I don't think so. So naturally I left him. I almost got an annulment. It was that bad—almost an annulment—but I said okay, okay, I'll settle for a nice little divorce. With the happy result was, I found your father. He didn't scream, he didn't yell, he laughed a lot, he didn't brag but a good provider. He stood up straight. He never said die. Naturally, of course, he wasn't perfect. He played cards, he gambled. He took me for granted. That was like a little gamble all by itself. You mean to tell me your cute little wife with that mean little heart of hers didn't live up to all your expirations?" She pushed a bowl of fruit my way across the

56

table. Long years of target practice had developed her motor skills. Black grapes tumbled; a few strays rolled across the floor, coming to rest where they might mature slowly into raisins or quickly into shoe mush. "So I'd like to know. What excuse you got, leaving that very nervous person?"

"I'm not happy with my wife."

"*Happy?*"

"It's not possible."

She beamed across the table a glare of disgust, fury, and sympathy. The disgust and fury were for my stupidity. She added a little knockout ray—*who is this son of mine?* The sympathy was for the fruit I had spurned. A few grapes got scrambled in her hand like my father blessing a pair of dice. "Give me the true story," she said. "Tell me what really goes on. Another girl? A shiksa with freckled legs? I suspected it all the time."

"Not now, it's not that, not now. It makes me feel no good to talk about it."

"Make yourself feel better. Talk about it. Is she pretty at least? Blond, like I was? At least I don't have all those funny little freckles they get."

"No, mother, don't—"

"You think I didn't learn the old American sayings? Love is blond."

My father was reading his paper and waiting for dinner. He might speak and he might not. He might be remembering when my mother had ash-colored pretty hair. He might be remembering it used to be important. Or he might be simply reading the paper, news of Ike and Sherman Adams and Francis Gary Powers.

He switched on the radio and switched it off. He switched on the television and switched it off. Well, they all worked. Sometimes he started his Olds at dawn to make sure it would work later, when he asked it to. He liked the news of the world because it could be ignored. It lay there in the newspaper and he had a choice about it. He liked to be self-reliant, but he also liked to be served his meals on time.

Part of self-reliance was not to get nervous when his wife sloped into one of her scientific exploration of reality moods, where she asked questions and offered answers. He had already passed through his nervousness about me and come out the other side. For one parent I was a grown son. He waited until I asked what he thought or until I asked for his help.

My younger brother, Sid, was ready to walk with me. It was our fraternal habit to walk the streets of Cleveland, investing neighborhoods with the turbulence and mystery of New York and Paris—strangers lived here, and also men like us, and also boys like the ones we used to be and re-mained with each other. As we grew older, we went on making plans for the future, as we always had, as if the future remained impenetrable and we remained seventeen and I didn't have a wife and children. My still younger brothers didn't care what I was doing or not doing with a family.

Our mother, however, needed news fresh off the plane for her sisters—especially for Anna—my aunts with hot dialing fingers, who were ringing and ringing to ask why this son, unlike their much better sons, should eat airline food and leave his woman. They pressed home with the Right to Inquire. And if she didn't know the whole story, how could she tell them the truth? She would have to guess —this would be vicious. The truth as I reported it and she interpreted it was so much more sisterly for her sisters, this judge and jury and grieving executioner squad, who had always warned her that boys who leave Cleveland get into trouble, sure as shooting. It wasn't their fault if she had let me go. They had warned her. Perhaps daily, while the standing rib and potatoes were roasting and boiling, they had lifted telephones against the sea of troubles. Their own sons picked brides from the local greenhouses, tended and watered under controlled circumstances—nice humid brides, fit for an intelligent person. Not her son. Thought he was smart. Not Frieda's son.

My mother had listened to them, but I had not listened to her.

I fell silent. I wasn't talking. Silence is a positive act and was taken as such. She drummed her fingers on the table.

"Dinnertime," my father remarked. He gave me the wink of a grizzled Marine rescuing a scout under fire. "Five minutes late already."

This was true. Only the deepest feelings would derail dinner. Into the breach leapt the mother. My brothers sat with their spoons in their fists, waiting for soup developments. They were ravenous at five minutes after six. Internal mechanisms had been detonated. The beast is trained to be alert to its needs, the turning of the sun, the moon, the tides, the evening news.

"It's mushroom barley vegetable potato minestrone tonight," my mother said. "I added the ingredients. Anybody say a cheer for that?" And to me, with intense fair warning: "After dinner you'll talk."

At table we performed the man's task. It happened that we had busy metabolisms, active appetites, and a never-requited yearning for the might of meat, the enticement of sweet. My father practiced a dreamy concentration when he was hungry. His sons did no less. The geography of nutrition entranced us, the rivers of gravy, avalanches of button mushrooms, the butter sunrises spreading over succotash jungles; yes, this family ate its vegetables. My youngest brother, Bob, muttered, "Pardon my reach," because it wasn't good manners to get grabby.

Another brother, Eugene, the lawyer, said, "Keep your elbows out of my salad."

"I *said* pardon my reach, didn't I?"

"I *said* your elbows are in my salad."

"Not anymore they're not," said a mother who wanted peace and harmony to welcome home the first divorcer among her children. "So shut up," she added with impartial hospitality. Neatly she flicked a piece of cucumber from my brother's sleeve into her palm, and then into a vessel waiting nearby for anonymous debris, chewed bones, rinds, crusts. "That Kraft's French dressing isn't too sticky, is it?" she asked, not having previously experienced its power to patch cucumber to arm. "This is a taste treat, lots of vitamins and roughage, isn't it?" she asked. "Do I hear a thank-you for the cook? I heard a burp—say scuse me—but now I want to hear a thank-you."

"Aw, thank you. Why aren't there any radishes today?"

The team of Good Eaters saw a job and did it. We performed pot roasticide and extreme canned-fruit Jell-O mold erosion, but deep within, hidden from our public, lay a secret resolution never to be fat. Pure will sometimes works in such cases. Our mother presided over the center of the earth with the Spirit of Nourishment. Here there would be no famine for her sons, and there was none.

The business at hand was eating and my divorce. One of my cousins had recently won a Nobel Prize, but this was bigger because closer to home—he wasn't a first cousin—and it was more pathetic, more tragic, more aggravating, more a thing not done in Cleveland; or if done, was quickly put under layers of forgetfulness and shushing, as her own divorce had been—practically not a marriage at all, no children, a pharmacist, a what-you-call-it, almost an annulment, it never was, it wasn't, it didn't. He was not so much a pharmacist as a druggist and it was a long time ago. The statute of limitations on whispers and telephone explorations of the case had expired. She submitted this incident for dismissal. She herself had dismissed it before I was born.

"I see by the papers Bill Veeck might sell the Indians," my father said. "So who cares?"

He slid sideways into silence. He had done his bit for table conversation. Important matters came to occupy his soul during these years—his age, the many years, his sons growing up and out, his business, his fading grasp of things, his intense sense of his fading. But during the meal he studied my face. I avoided his gaze so he wouldn't be driven to speak of Bill Veeck and the Cleveland Indians. He had learned to use baseball a little like an American—a jangle to occupy the emptiness of summer. I knew one of the things he wanted for me tonight—to help me filter the high beams of my mother's intentions—and I appreciated his thought.

"Watch what you're doing," my mother said. "Look what I made. How come you're not trying the beets?"

How come, she meant to ask, you're not eating everything at once? The soup, the salad, the pot roast with peas, the beets, the A & P ice cream, made with milk and chemicals because they say fat isn't as good for people as it used to be, the homemade apple pie, berry pie, peach pie—no sugar, hardly any, a little bit just for taste—the coffee with milk because, well, milk is the best food going, no matter what they say. And when it was all done, a question: "Who's going to help me finish this tiny bit of soup? I ain't got no room in the box. Who likes a little mushroom barley Italian potato vegetable minestrone soup before I throw it out? Going, going—"

Fat chance. Always room in the box. Nobody wanted a little soup after the three kinds of pie with thin civilian ice cream. Strong enough we brothers were for normal life in America, earning a living, military service, but not quite mighty enough at table.

By this time the beets had mysteriously been added to the soup. My mother was the Houdini of food consolidation.

My brother said he would make his own coffee. He had names for the local product: Revenge of the Caffeine Monster, Postum From Outer Space, Sanka Claws.

"Okay, okay," mother said. "But you listen to the doctors: strong coffee hurts the nerves. Try to get smart. If one of you turned out a doctor, you'd know."

"I know," said Sid.

"Then do what you want," my mother said. "Here, cream? Sugar?"

"Black," said my brother, and my mother shivered. But she knew her sons were independent in their own ways.

Sid carried his cup into the backyard, under the pear tree our mother had planted. In good weather we all liked to visit her garden. She grew flowers, tomatoes, sweet peas, other vegetables, a Victory Garden before and after it was a patriotic duty. It was a place where she sometimes fell silent. The mysteries of this domestic corner made us understand there was more to her than we knew, more to the earth, sky, and sun, more to the moon and stars, more to ourselves, too. Sid sat leaning against the pear tree, sipping coffee and smoking his pipe. My father and other brothers cleared out of the kitchen. Mother's turn for depth interrogation was near; it was here. Justification in such cases is unnecessary yet imperative. She was alone with her eldest son. She sought the proper diplomatic way to frame the third degree.

"So what you said was, you weren't satisfied with your wife," she began, in case my memory needed refreshment. She wiped her hands on an apron which wasn't there, in her distraction wiping her hands on her skirt. "Sit down now, sit down, stop packing around, sit still a minute, you're not a hockey player anymore, you're a happily married man, and tell me what or why and how come you say you weren't satisfied with the wife you chose for love in this free country. She's still cute, isn't she?"

We don't have confession and priests. We don't have closed booths. We don't have even one Hail Mary. We have the kitchen table. I felt the breath tight in my chest. I said, "She wasn't happy with me, either."

"The truth will out, won't it?"

My brother was waiting under the pear tree. My father was turning the knobs on the TV. I would have preferred to be elsewhere.

"Don't want to complain anymore," I said.

Mother shook her head. "I wasn't sure I never liked her," she said. "Tell me how mean she was. Get a load off—you look worn down. Tell me about the laws in your state. How long before it's final, you can date again, you can find a nice wife with a good nature this time and raise a nice family—two families for you, shlimazl. Not that I don't like the only grandchildren I got so far."

"I'm not thinking so far ahead yet. But I can what you call date."

"What you call it then? Sleep-around? Not that I blame

you, your health needs a little—I never enjoyed her so much."

Suddenly I looked up in response to some strange motion in the air; it came from the doorway; it was a disturbance of my father's eyebrows, speckled black fur rustling invisible currents into the screened stuff we were breathing. He was standing in the doorway and grinning. His mouth was huge. His eyebrows were working. As soon as I caught his eye, he winked; and then he went back to the newspaper and the TV, studying today's news of the cold war—the Cold War, as it was called.

"You got something to say about our son the married man having dates?" she called to him. She cupped her ear. No answer.

The wink was gone, but I had taken it into my secret store of happinesses and gratitudes, along with the Russian bath where we used to steam and have Sunday breakfast, broiled liver on wooden trays, men decked in towels for company.

Misery was my chief occupation now. I paid attention to the insistent distress being beamed my way by a person who only had my welfare at heart. "Okay," she said, "what's important? You want me to tell you or you want to listen?"

The summer light was fading. My father crossed twice through the kitchen, then went to bed. My walking brother, the king of the walkers of Cleveland, smoked his pipe and waited under the pear tree. If I wasn't walking tonight, jet-lagged, lagged by mother, he would go alone. He knew my habit—to give our mother her talk first, then live a little. As darkness fell over Cleveland, over Cleveland Heights, Shaker Heights, Euclid Heights, over the hillsides and lakefront, over Taylor Road with its whoosh of traffic, over the mountain-high memories of Cleveland, and my mother sat waiting for a little nice conversation about grief from me, her eldest son, and I sat waiting for something from her, my only mother, it seemed to me that her body was swelling and filling with midearth lava in the kitchen; this tiny plump woman was growing huge and might explode, bringing convulsion and ruin. I remembered coming home late from school, and my shame because I knew I had wanted to be late, wanted to play hockey and not to go shopping for winter clothes during the sales; I remembered forgetting to practice the piano, and denying I had decided not to practice the piano anymore; I remembered her anxious staring at me when I crept in, shoeless and mussed, after late nights with friends who drank beer at seventeen.

Now in the silence there were no twistings of the tongue. Suddenly her eyes filled with tears and she said, "It's hard, son, isn't it?"

"Ma, it is."

"I used to say someday you'd understand. Now you do."

I didn't answer—*understand what?*—and in this rare and marvelous silence she added, "You don't have to answer. You don't have to tell me."

"That's right, ma."

"Now you can go for a walk with your brother. Or if you want to, your dad wouldn't mind, wake him up and sit."

I went to do one of those things, accepting my release. Mother turned off the light, but she didn't leave the room. I looked back. She sat in the dark. I used to wonder if she dreamed, if she dreamed of some other life, if she dreamed of her past, if like others she imagined something sweet which never existed. Now she sat in the dark, my mother sat dreaming in the dark. The tireless lady whose voice flowed on and on, like a wind in a canyon, like a force of endless rustling nature, fell silent in the dark. What did she think of at four-thirty in the morning when she stood sorting at the laundry machine while my father lay submerged in his uneasy old man's groaning doze? What did she think of now in the dark, as she contemplated my divorce and her grandchildren, as she thought of what to do next, as she considered baking or bulk bleach or sons, with that loose-fleshed tide of age slipping over her body? She could not have told me and I could not wrench her privacy from her. It was not available. What I saw was the sadness. If I had asked, the torrent of words would have begun again. Within a mere torrential insistence of words she hid herself. With sad and eager eyes, she set straight the world and her son. But now in the silence what she sent out with abrupt solid force was simply unknowable loneliness, nothing more.

As a child, I used to rise secretly out of my bed, creeping through the house to discover her at her tasks. I inherited her habit of night living, predawn living. She had forbidden me to read so much, ruins the eyes, so I hid books under my mattress and read by the first blue cracks of daylight when nobody was watching me ruin my eyes. The clack of hooves on country roads brings back memories of the books I read in Lakewood, Ohio. Tarzan, the Ted Scott adventures, and the Bible—whatever came my way under the mattress before breakfast, when I moved on to the backs and sides of cereal boxes. I still remember how Lord Greystoke learned to decipher letters in the jungle, and how Ted Scott crossed the ocean alone in his biplane, and how Delilah sneaked up on Samson in the dark and bit off his hair. When I crunched Grapenuts, I also read about how they were crunchy. The living proof that words give fair information about the world.

There were milk deliveries by horse-drawn wagon until the war. Twittering sparrows followed the traces of the horses, selectively cleaning up. I tucked Tarzan back under the mattress and pretended to stretch and awaken. "School-time!" Breakfasttime! Wash your face!" In those days my strict mother, seeking to save me from blindness, seemed old, but she was much younger than I am today; her hair was pale.

When I spied at her in the dark where she now sat considering not eyestrain but divorce, her hair was still faintly pale, blond as it had been when she was a girl and before it darkened and thinned and she took to wearing a Korean wig in public for beauty's sake. When I said, "Don't wear that thing," she always answered, "What *thing?* Your dad's side got the good hair in this family. You got the thick hair like your father. I got the rabbis, the scholars, the doctors—okay, so he happened by accident to have one the Noble Prize. What *thing* you call it? I got the thin hair."

She didn't mention the grayness. Did I want her to dye her hair like a chorus girl? Like the woman she had seen one of my cousins with—on my father's side? Better to wear the nice Korean wig, like a lady.

Her hair was normal for her age, gray and wispy and autumnally dry, but now in the blurring dark it seemed thick and rich. She was sad beyond what we said to each other. This is a characteristic of sadness between friends and lovers or among family, no matter how the poets and complainers try to put things right, no matter how mothers wail and sons grumble and lovers demand. There is sadness which is utter, irreducible, and the words which comfort are also claws that deceive and wound.

She was not moving. Slowly that first night of my visit she was shaking her head at ghosts.

Reconciliation in families is always partial and for a moment. Recognition and devotion are not enough. Nothing is enough. The past exists without further plan, like the will of the deceased. My mother sat hiccupping in the dark and I walked away from her tears, as she knew I would.

The next morning, waking early and stupefied by time changes, I prepared for an appointment with the family lawyer-accountant. My father recommended this, I obeyed, my mother insisted, I repeated, "But I'm going, don't *tell* me to go, I'm *going*, mother."

"Every little bit helps," she said, serving scrambled eggs.

"You asked me what I wanted. I said softboiled or poached."

"Today I made scrambled," she said.

"Then why did you ask?"

"You're a guest in my house."

The formerly married man forked up the heavy, brownish eggs, thinking not about what she called "egg omelets" but about driving downtown. I took the keys and said, "No, I won't lose them—how could I lose them?" The eggs were heavy, brown, and slick. A guest, an eldest son bringing shame and divorce to Cleveland, doesn't quibble over his breakfast and shouldn't complain at being reminded not to drop the car keys on the sidewalk where they can be snatched up by hit-and-run muggers.

"Come back and tell us what Grossman says," she called. "That woman shouldn't take you for all you got, not that you got anything. You don't have to give her an astrological sum or amount so she can buy more and more cashmere, that Person lamb we gave her was enough. Drive careful. Turn the key to start it. Park in the lot down on Rockwell. They validate. Don't forget to validate. I'll make a good lunch, you come back, don't go wandering around—you want a snack in case you got to wait?"

My divorce and the scrambled eggs troubled me all the

way down from Cleveland Heights into the flatlands in the steady rush-hour traffic. So this is commuting; this is normal life, these morose, morning-swollen, Cleveland faces of those who drove downtown every day, digesting their own eggs and toast through the nonaerobic exercise of stopping and going and keeping in lane.

I parked in the lot on Rockwell. The details for Mr. Grossman weighed heavily. The paperwork. The breakfast. I would do what I had to do.

I sat in front of a glass-topped desk, oppressed in heart and belly, weighted, freighted, feeling I should take a pen and check some figures but not knowing what the figures might be. The lawyer-accountant was small and brown, with a knobby nose stuck on his face by his Maker at the last possible moment, probably as he left the assembly line— probably late on a Friday afternoon. He hummed and moved his lips as he looked through a manila folder. "That's all?" he asked. "Now let's see about your holdings."

My mother's scrambled eggs, converted into cargo, were shifting ominously in their container. "No holdings, what's holdings?" I asked.

"Okay, I see no real estate or stock, how about savings? GI insurance?"

"Yes. Policy in my daughters' names for benefits."

"That's it?"

The eggs were fomenting revolution down below. Chagrin and yellowness seeped through weakening defenses, then flooded and soared from stomach to brain.

"Your wife, your ex, your soon-to-be former, she's—um —she just got crazy or she got somebody else or it's alimony, spousal support we call it, she desires?"

I stood up, teetered on my palms against the cool glass top of the desk, knew cool palms would not save me, ran into the hall. I leaned and my head split open and my stomach fired up eggs, bile, green, brown, a mess of running mice and floodtide debris onto a hallway lined with glass doors for lawyers, accountants, wholesalers, mail orderers, and the Felicity Christian Missionary Research Inc. Foundation.

"Oh, God," I said, feeling amazed as my prayer seemed to cause the Felicity Christian people to open their door, peer out briefly, and slam shut. The foundation's missionary activity extended to savage blacks and browns, which evidently did not necessarily include my shade of liverish yellow. Oh God, oh God, I said, striving, leaning against the mottled marble walls. I was taking both my divorce and my breakfast too hard. It wasn't real marble. Maybe my life and my stomach were not a real tragedy. But one felt arid and stony hard, the other boiling and final. Mr. Grossman, the lawyer-accountant, emerged and put his little freckled hand on my shoulder while he leaned, ungainly, to keep his shoes out of range. "I'm sorry," he said, "I guess this gets sort of aggravating, not used to domestic relations like this, are you? I'll call maintenance."

"Okay." I was gasping and crumpled.

"You want to finish our conference another day? No hurry, lad. You feel better now?"

"Okay."

"Go home, have a nice lunch, rest, dry toast, rice, broth or bouillon, your mother knows best—"

He had stamped my validation. At least that was a plus. I drove with finicky care, observing the brown and sepia world through hepatic misery. Cleveland looked like old snapshots, with deckled edges, but moved strangely, even made honks and oogas, brown screeches and brown static. I was glad for slow traffic if not for much else. I still tasted an eggishness soaked into my flesh. I had only eaten two, I thought, but there seemed to be many, the eggs of ancient carrion birds, crackling in the light and air.

I parked my parents' automobile—an Olds it was—and headed past my mother to bed, one step following the next. "What did Grossman advise? How much you giving her? You're touching the walls with your smeary hands," she said, "why is that?"

"Don't feel well."

"Such is obvious. You got a letter from your wife. I can't help it I still call her your wife, that woman. Why didn't she use the phone, dial direct, we could talk, I'm the only mother-in-law she got?"

"Where's the letter?"

"I opened it in case something important—"

"Mother!"

"Why read it in your weakened condition? Have a nap first, you want some tea?"

"Mother! You opened my letter?"

She shook her head, which normally might mean no, but said, "Just nagging is all she got on her mind." She handed me the sheets. There was food on them—she must have balanced reading my mail with lunch preparation. "Wouldn't take her too serious. Just trying to get your goat is all. It's well-known in such cases."

She shot maternal inoculation looks to protect me from the eloquent but harsh arguments of a recent spouse. The drawing weakness in my belly joined the crazy anger in my head to fashion a very sleepy person, a baby boy with upset stomach, urgently needing to close his eyes for beddybye at noon.

"You don't want lunch?" my mother asked. "You're going to your room to read what *that person* thinks she got

71

to say to you, no good sense at all plus a funny handwriting which it slants the wrong way? You spend your time reading her letter and not even tasting a nice salad, some boiled potato from last night, a little cheese, a little cold pot roast, I'll warm it up, a few beets in minestrone soup? You want I should bring you a tray, you feel so rotten about what that woman does to you?"

I managed myself into pajamas. It was like dressing another person, boneless and retarded. There was relief in sliding between cool sheets in the boy's bed that used to be mine, before college, the war, and marriage. As the quarrel between gravity and my stomach subsided, I could concentrate on the crankcase experience of my mouth. The brain was still clogged.

Mother stood in the doorway, looking at the sheets of letter on the floor. They were black with divebombing rows of Stuka words. "So read, I suppose you want, then I'll bring a tray," she said. How could we discuss without food and full disclosure? No wonder she had to study the letter first. She watched me taking long gulps of bedroom air. She remarked, "Don't feel so good?"

"Sick."

"Maybe I put too much bacon grease in the eggs. But you got so skinny, due to martial strife."

"What bacon grease?"

"You know we don't keep kosher. I was out of chicken fat lately."

"You scrambled those eggs with a lot of bacon grease?"

"Maybe half a cup, no more, give it that nice brown color. A little nourishment for you, skin and bones, you ever eat anymore?"

Opened my mail. Dosed my eggs. Didn't listen. Fury and despair and a new peristaltic quaking in my belly.

A fever of outrage burned my forehead, but there was no way to employ this heat. Belly crisis pushes to the front of the line, easily disposing of revenge. I might want to tell her pure hatred—*how could you? how could you?*—but in a state of gut and flux, I could only ask her for oblivion.

"Turn off the light, ma. I have to sleep now."

This mother took pride in her discretion, tact, and anticipation of a son's needs. She did not say it was too early in the day for a nap, especially without lunch. I sank, cuddling peacefully with injustice. I tumbled head over belly into fadeout, hearing sympathetic and compassionate moans in the doorway, "Poor boy, poor boy, poor son of mine," while she checked out the peculiar color of my face and reread the pages scattered on the floor. "So upset can't digest his good breakfast—why do people have to do like this to other people?"

I came awake at midnight. A summer drizzle slipped down from the slate sky. It cooled things off. The window sweated droplets; they slid without a sound to the wooden edge of the screen. Most of the remaining bacon oil had passed through my filtration equipment. In the bathroom mirror my eyes looked scraped and red, as if I had been weeping in my sleep for lost love, past gone, present going, the snowfall of endless letter still surrounding the bed I had slept in as a child. But my skin was no longer brown with liverspill. I went into the kitchen, looking for something sharp—oh, grapefruit juice, say, or an orange or lemon—to cut through tastes for which I had no further use.

Usually at this hour my mother slept. She would get up later, perhaps at three or four. But now at midnight she was still sitting in the dark. "Don't turn on the light," she said, "sometimes even the switch awakens your father. Sometimes he's too delicate. You probably take after him—nervous stomach."

She wanted to make progress between us. She had told me about her mother, her wonderful mother, who died while her daughter was pregnant and never had the chance to diaper the grandson, me. She had tried to form an American of my grandfather, who refused to learn English because he already knew Russian, Polish, Yiddish, and Hebrew, which covered the known world plus heaven. He also refused to work in the land of plenty because he had studied to be something other than a drunken American. In America he prayed in the synagogue and played checkers, and although his entire family disagreed with this course of action, he was stubborn. Like me, of course. The men on all sides in this family were stubborn. She listed her sisters, counting them off on her fingers, saving Aunt Anna for her biggest finger, who had also tried to knock their husbands into shape; not much luck. Then she reviewed my father: "He's a good provider. But he thinks the children are my business. And he doesn't listen, you notice? Sometimes he acts like he's deaf. You think he can't hear or he doesn't want to?"

She had told me all this. She told me again.

"But a good provider he is. Only if he wasn't so pigheaded. So why don't you let me put some sugar on the grapefruit? How can you eat it like that? So sour, it'll make your teeth sore. A little sugar and you're so skinny anyways, skinny and bones these days like it is."

I kept the peace. It was the sacred hour of midnight. When next I ate an egg, I would prepare it myself.

"Tell me something about where you live," she said. "There's lots of sissies? I read in the paper all the sissies go there."

"Mother, there are homosexuals everywhere."

"Sha!" she cried. "Watch your language. Try to remember I'm your mother."

"Are you asking if I'm one?"

She knocked on wood. A man who allows himself to be divorced might try anything, not that I wasn't better off without this specific wife. But still, the children. And the family, the neighbors, the friends who sold bonds with her, the ghost of my grandmother, who put up with terrible problems from a lazy greenhorn husband—what explanation was there?

I had no answer to history. Her world was some Atlantis kingdom, midway between Russia and America. In ways I had yet to understand, this realm was also mine, links of bewilderment and longing locking us together. My mother sat in the dark with sad eyes and uttered her best truth to whatever ear might listen. "I'm looking back, back, back so far to see what happened to you," she said in her kitchen which smelled of soap and onions and a used banana, smelled of fear that she may have led her son astray. She put doubt behind her, a talent she had; the banana ripeness persisted, with Fels naphtha and vegetable bite. "We were happy with the little God gave us—we took from him. If we were unhappy, other people, not our own family, made us that way. So answer."

"This is America," I said. It was an answer I had learned years ago when I didn't quite understand her questions. Also I suspected her piety; God usually came to her aid when she wanted to make an important point. "We got everything in America, including things we don't want."

"You think I wasn't raised here? You think I don't know your misery, you other Americans? I vote, too. I pick up the paper from my front porch, just like I was born here. I was born here enough to speak English before you did, and to say ouch! when you were born—you think you came clean? You came dirty like anybody else. You think I'm not your mother and you're my oldest son? Who a-nominated and elected you oldest boy?" She stirred in the summer dark; skycast reflections, the steady slate glow of rain, her turbulent flowing and rustling in her chair. Anger over me always put her into action again, reliving my birth, saying ouch. Nothing incited her so richly as suspecting I was ungrateful, withdrawn, or pissed, and that she might have helped to make me so. "And about that wife of yours—she dared! Like a princess in her own mind! An idea she has! The last thing I could do with your father is dare to be unhappy." She whispered, "He won't allow it. I think maybe he's a stronger fella than you are"—she relented—"so far, son. Don't worry. You got time. Certain prophets were just about dying at your age"—still relenting, shifting down—"but you got plenty of time."

"I'm not worried about that," I said. "I'm not dying."

"Thanks God."

"I'm not a prophet either."

"In that case, worry a little. It's not so terrible to make plans, even be disappointed sometimes in your New Year's resolution." She was breathing so shallowly it was like a shiver. "You don't necessarily mind what I say. That's always how you been, since you were a little kid. Spoiled, stubborn, and spoiled, but what you used to do in the old days was you used to digest good. I fed you on mother's milk, and then lots of fruit Jell-O, protein, soup, only good things. Now what? A bad stomach on top of a bad wife. So what happens next? What could?"

She settled there amid the new square milk cartons and bottles for grease storage; she settled amid spicy vegetables that dry in a kitchen, garlic, brown and pimpled onions

with green sprouts very unlike their host, parsnips, tur-
nips, radishes, roots my father liked to slice in the sink and
eat with a little chicken fat on a Sunday afternoon. Her
bottom flowed over the chair, her worry flowed over her
face, the eyes showed few doubts—she saw to that. Puzzle-
ment remained like a root, sprouting worries. How could
such a son get himself in such a fix? With all the good food
and advice she had ladled out, why hit with both a divorce
and a delicate stomach? Why unhappy, why hit with that?
Why still needing love and not getting it?

Why couldn't I take the good of a mother's cooking and
care for me? Concern seized me by the hair and flung me
down, but it was love all the same, it was how this mother
served it. She studied me in the dark.

"Son, sometimes I was burning," the voice continued.
"There was no answer, always used to be other things on
his mind, but I kept on living like a wife with your father.
What's the good of getting crazy on other people? By myself sometimes I got a little crazy in the middle of the night,
when the cooking and the cleaning is there to be done
anyway, and who knows the difference in the daylight if a
crazy person did it while they slept?"

Sometimes, and just now, beneath the familiar rhythms
of maternal aria, I heard another rhythm, that of silence, of
her blood throbbing, of her body which had issued forth its
sons and no daughters and therefore lacked for company in
this family of boys and men. She had her sister Anna at the
reach of the telephone. She tried to be girl and grandmother
and herself, all at once, because she wanted something more
amid the faulted bounty of her male brood. When she arose
early, she was searching company in the quiet of her house.
At dawn in the summer, before dawn in the winter, she did
the laundry and baked cookies, no sugar, lots of raisins,
maybe a little sugar after all, and sometimes listened at my

father's door to his nightmares. She never discovered his secrets; he could not know hers; they both sensed a loss. So she opened letters—was it less foolish than trying to imagine what dear ones think and dream? Her hands still now, but not at rest in her lap, stilled by an act of grasping, she tried to make me understand. "I never had time with all you boys growing up and your father needing me, I never had time to study how the butterflies sniff the flowers, or if they do. Maybe only the bees drink from flowers. How would I know? I had to wait. I always had to wait."

She needed to be sensible. She didn't have time to be a crazy person. Could one of us understand this? One of her family?

She had counseled patience to me before, but never claimed it for herself. She had never counseled disappointment. Her hands looked empty and weary. Usually they were sewing, cooking, admonishing. She had always promised hard work would be rewarded. But maybe a marriage isn't supposed to be just hard work, her marriage or mine.

"I met your father"—I already knew this—"we were ice skating at the rink on Euclid, City Ice & Fuel. He was funny and smart and my sister knew him, she recommended him, a good provider." Her skin emitted the smells of damp grass and the wet earth of a garden—a healthy old woman's smell. In this garden of puffy ankles and swollen joints there had once been an ice skater's grace. "We was first married, your father used to take out the rubbish without I had to ask him. You adjust to everything, son, and this zero darkness we got here, too." She reached across the table to touch my face. She let her hand fall when I was startled. "But there got to be advantages someplace. Your stomach, I'm glad it's better."

5 BEFORE DAWN one winter morning in San Francisco the telephone shrilled down over a dream forever lost. His hand snaked out, followed by some corner of mind, followed by blinking eyes. *Hello? Hello? Hello?*

"It's—"

It was his former wife ringing in the dark. Imagining accident, illness, disaster, some horror about their children, he stammered and shouted, "What's wrong! What's wrong!"

Her pealing laughter by telephone from elsewhere—laughter he had once found dear.

"What's wrong?" he said.

She laughed and laughed while he waited. "I forgot, it's somewhat earlier out there, isn't it?" she asked. There were fog horns blowing. The night was wet on the window. Then she remarked, "Nothing. I'm leaving my husband. I want to talk with you in person, it's really important, of the utmost. And they need to see you."

"Don't decide anything yet," he said. *They* meant the children this laughing voice and he had given the world and each other during a time which lay in the past like old snapshots stored in a box. "I'll be there today," he said.

Dressing, he considered what he wanted to utter, like a boy rehearsing a speech. *We can be friends, but not good friends.* It seemed unctuous, but bad theater has a place in life. He went back for rewriting: cut not *good* friends, try not *close* friends. He pulled on his socks in the morning chill and tried: *Your husband's a fine man, don't do it.* That sounded even more unctuous, sententious, and pompous, but advice-giving tends to grow heavy in rehearsal. He might lighten up after breakfast.

He called United Airlines as the sky turned orange beneath the fog and the electric pot mumbled. Sometimes pompous sententious unctuous nonsense might be the best approach to connections between people who are no longer connected. Bad theater and melodrama also reflect realities.

And yet, their blood mingled in two daughters, they would always be connected. This was the mother of his children. This was the woman he had chosen. He threw the dufflebag over his shoulder; he pulled the door shut and doublelocked it. *Of the utmost*, he thought. He was on his way to her again.

He needed his children, but the cause of his visit was their mother. To cross the continent was easy; to cross Detroit, low, flat, brown, clogged arteries and tangles of traffic, was slow. One daughter hugged and kissed with the shyness of the months which somehow pass. The other daughter hung back and watched; her eyes were suspicious, asking to be convinced. He gave his daughters the barrettes he had bought in the San Francisco airport gift shop. They looked at the pictures of ponytails on the cardboard. Dick Clark Teensomes for Today. They murmured polite thank-yous.

The mother greeted him with the smiling ease of an old lover now making firm decisions on a regular basis. There were gracious wiggles in her welcome. She drew the carpeting, the curtains, the silver, the furniture into the orbit of hello, but she liked also *not* to care about these things. The world of ideas and spirit was what really mattered, not good taste, even if she couldn't help filling some of the idle hours with distinctive Danish Modern goods, Marimekko, Design Research. Her husband was away in his office. She needed to talk, or rather, to explain and ratify.

He had practiced his portion of the conversation so many times during a day in an airplane that he felt like an actor in a stock company. He would try to wait for his cues, looking his partner in the eye, or at least in the bridge of her small nose, and then speak his lines.

"Would you like to go out for coffee?"

"Yes, sure. Are the kids all right left alone?"

"They're getting older, my dear. You're not around to see how nice they're getting."

"I'm here as often as I can—"

"Of course you are. Whenever you can, whenever it's convenient. I know a place serves a great cappuccino in the afternoon, steamed milk really hot, and since you sprung for the airplane, I'll spring for the coffee—"

Since she so much wanted to, he let her spring. They sat smiling at each other over a table which was almost of marble on spindly wrought iron. He remembered the genuine formica and vinyl bench booths they used to sit at when they were graduate students making plans for eternity, for work, travel, children, and romance unending. Their divorce had been a jagged and brutal amputation. He thought it was now seared shut. He lived far away; he was pleased to be there. Talking with her, he felt both anxious and curious. He'd have given up satisfying the curiosity in favor of not reviving the anxiety, hammered and seared and finally, blessedly, welded down, closed, interred, shrunk, beaten, by God—

"Let's assume I've said all the polite things and you've made all the polite answers," his former wife stated happily. "And now I'll get to the point."

This woman he almost knew, used to know, didn't know at all, explained what she had worked out in her head during these several years of unmarriage, particularly during the past few months. It turned out their divorce was an error. Errors can be rectified, else they become mistakes; or perhaps it is mistakes which must be rectified to avoid error. At any rate, the former couple needed each other. It was clear to her now. Did he understand how everything had changed, become clear, was now revealed? He was the one after all! She invited him to be pleased at a compliment suddenly unveiled—she intended it, and didn't it make him happy? Praise never hurts. Sincere praise never hurts even more. Yes, another cappuccino, please; without the sprinkles of chocolate, please.

She was elaborating a spell; her hands were making complex weaving motions in an air smelling of coffee and sweets. Here was the plan: to leave her present temporary husband—oh, just a reaction he was—and take up again where they had been and still belonged as dear loving spouse and spouse, as a couple the perfect couple, no not that but so much wiser because we've learned so much these difficult years so hard now I realize . . . at the utmost. . . . Of course, there would be a period of lovely shy courtship, art movies, long walks, discussions, just like old times—

There were bits of grit in his throat, but he avoided clearing it. Throat-clearing tends to spoil the tender art movie, long walk, basic discussion mood. He said through lumps and grits, "We can be friends. I'm really pleased about that. But not close friends."

She beamed and touched his wrist. She knew he needed time. She forgave a certain dullness, a *manqué d'entrain*. She was willing to go far, just as she had offered to spring for the coffee. She had more than forgiven his slow thinking; she knew how to convert it into a necessary bridge. "You don't understand?" she asked.

"And your husband's a nice man, much better for you than I could be. I envy his luck to have won you."

"But you're missing the point! I've changed my mind!"

With this little speech she pulled the cloth off the monument, she blessed the sculptor, she inaugurated a new era. They were united again, slim versions of a Maillol "Fecundity." "I see it all differently now—the way it used to be!"

He wished these words not to float around unmatched. Yet it would be irrelevant to mention his own condition and vision. His intentions for himself would only confuse her. That was not the issue. The conversation must never leave her interests. People make such unnecessary complications, always thinking of themselves and not of her. Oh, it's hard to speak, he thought. And he also thought: *Say something.* Playing for time, he said, "It's nice we can be good friends now. Not just for the children, but for us. Would you like a refill? Another cappuccino?"

She lit a cigarette and blew steadily into his face. He tried breathing shallowly—not to cough, not to complain—while he admired her brilliance, a champion-class stubborn nimbleness, how she passed through panic in a few seconds, how she refused to let anything be what she didn't want it to be. This talent even extended to uncosmic matters. If God happened to ask, she would state in all sincerity, "But I thought my nonsmoking former husband likes to have smoke blown in his face." If God asked, she would have said, "But I always thought he was only waiting for me to change my mind."

Since God neither asked nor answered, it was left to her to invent the world.

When reality penetrated the grand design, it went through a miracle transformation. It suited her, however it began. When she was sick, it turned out the world was mistaken in its definition of sickness. Sickness was health; wasn't that clear? Rearrangement was one of her many powers. All the great philosophers did this, though many of them were not so speedy, so confidential, so indulgent of others. Her large dark clever eyes shone; she shook her hair; she licked her lips—she was enthusiastic about her task, at least when she was enthusiastic about it. She could teach her former husband to be her next husband and to enjoy smoke blown in his face. In her system, with all her dramatic daring and subtlety, life could be disciplined to a classic movie, only spoken in American, without subtitles.

He coughed, she smiled, she had won one more tiny skirmish. Even for him it was better than all-out nuclear war. Since he had coughed, she handed him a paper napkin, in case he might need it.

They drove back from this tête-à-tête which had some of the form but not the content of the end of their marriage, those crazed low-voiced conversations in public places which gave them recreation from the crazed screaming conversations in the privacy of their own house. Her husband had a meeting downtown; they were lucky in the commuter traffic on the feeder roads; so far okay. A thought performed little loops of easy turmoil in his forehead; why did he feel no more relief than he used to feel in seeming to settle something for her?

Why did he think their divorce could ever be settled, since their marriage never was?

But it's finished, he thought. Once more.

There were still their daughters. Judy was pasting in her scrapbook. Ann was waiting for him. She wanted her private time. She was eleven and she wanted to talk with him like grownups. As her mom did, she wanted to go for a ride and a walk and a taste of something sweet. Important family business with her father, important discussion, important matters. She had a right. Family business was the procedure for running a family in which there were no sure procedures. She was wearing the barrette. She was glum and then talkative and even stopped licking her spoon, although strawberry sundaes were her favorite.

His elder daughter was talking too fast. It seemed she had memorized some lines, just as he had, but hers were more complicated, since they had been composed for her. He should move back home. Mom wanted to live with him again, she really did. The family should be together again, it really should, dad. Everything would be nice now, dad, it really would. . . .

The sadness of the mother in the child finally crackled through the scenarios of the day. He was startled and miserable. He discovered his former wife's genuine grief just when he was also enraged at putting their daughter out on stage, arranging her to do this work. He took deep breaths, hoped she couldn't hear the thumping in his chest, and resolved to speak slowly and patiently. "Mom's married," he said. "It's a nice husband. He's not your father, I'm still your dad. Look at me now. Look at me. I'll be with you always anyway, but he's her husband now—"

"You're in another city."

"I can buy airplane tickets. You come to see me vacations. We see each other a lot, and we can write and telephone—"

Her eyes filled with tears of frustration. It had been rehearsed and planned to be another way. "Not the same, dad!"

"I know."

"Not right, dad."

He tugged at her shoulder with his hand. She didn't move. He slid over and put his arms around her. "It's how things are, darling, it's not so bad—"

"But it is."

She was right and it was. In the diminished voice of shame he said, "Can't be changed like this. Can't go back anymore."

They ate ice cream and talked. He asked about school. She answered. Nothing much to say. About her friends. Nothing much on her mind. He hoped she would feel better. She said she felt fine.

She didn't feel fine.

He told her it was right to say what she felt, and especially what she really felt, that would be really good, not what another asked her to say. "Mom didn't tell me what to say."

"Okay." He felt rotten but did not tell her that.

"Okay, dad. Okay, then," she said. "Thanks for the barrette."

The next morning, when he came to see his daughters, their mother was marvelously alert. Everything seemed to have changed. Even the chairs were rearranged—there were fresh flowers on the table near the door. She danced across the room, arms extended. Her face was crackling with her happy laughter. Something had happened last night. She had an announcement to make. "I'm going to have a child," she sang out, "I've wanted another."

He asked no questions. He expressed nothing but an uncle's jolly satisfaction. He beamed, making chins. Whatever happened last night was none of his business. Even the discussion she had proposed with him was not really his business. He assumed she had not so much changed her mind as forgotten her other plan. That was only the reality of a few days ago. Act Ninety-Nine, he thought.

He needed no explanation. He would listen like an uncle. No, like a thrilled playgoer. He was Mister-First-Nighter. It was the glamor of endless risk and rescue, a damsel in distress and a prince riding up just in time. It was an entrancement! (He listened like a former husband in fear of his life.)

"You were right!" she cried. "He's a much better man than you. And now we're going to have a baby!"

"You and I can be awfully good friends," he said.

Eight years ago, down the winding Petionville road above Port-au-Prince, he had walked with his elder daughter. "Bougainvillea," he said.

"Bougain, villea," she answered.

"Donkey," he said.

"Donkey, daddy."

They had the naming of flowers and animals and the chasing of lizards. "Oh! Oh! More!" she said, running at the tiny green creatures which twitched, swelled up their dragon necks, and disappeared in a shiver. "More," she said, holding his hand.

The blood-red flowers.

The high-pitched chatter of the market ladies, carrying their burdens to town on their heads. The skinny black pigs, as rapid as dogs. The nibbling, nose-twitching goats, indifferent to the goatskins drying on a fence. The children crying, "Allo blanc!"

When a donkey did donkey dung near them, a steaming tumble beneath the parted pink flesh, grunts and heehaw, she said, "Daddy!" joyous with complicity in the joke. Nature is like this, he told her, and she answered, "Not me, daddy. I use the potty. My *sister* is like this."

They laughed and then they were silent and he smelled violent growth and sweet rot and this was a moment which redeemed everything in life. The child holding his hand. The names in French and Creole and English of lizards and donkeys and flowers. This day of white tropical sky, charcoal smoke, the teeming road, the buzzings and dartings and comfort of the child holding his hand.

Now on his way back across the continent, United Airlines #33, iced and dried in a tube through the abstract skies, he sat stupefied with the echo of his daughter talking so fast to him, using her own words for another's purpose, a willed manipulation throbbing like the shared blood through their arms as she held his hand, looking into his eyes and speaking what she was supposed to speak. The made-up, put-up chatter of a child did the bidding of misery and delusion. She wanted to hold his hand, she searched his eyes with longing, it was a child's longing and clinging; the words connived.

His younger daughter had said goodbye slyly, watching from the corners of her lovely dark eyes, wondering if he would ever do what he was supposed to do, what a real father would do—take charge. Instead, all he did was command her to look at him, hold her close, and go. When she began to undo his shoelaces, he said sharply, "Don't!" He was a goodbye daddy with airplane tickets sticking out of his pocket.

When the trays were buckled to their laps he didn't even flirt with the pretty young woman at his side. "You live in California?" she asked.

"Yes."

"In San Francisco?"

"Yes."

"You're always such a blabbermouth?"

She may have been a nervous person in an airplane or she may have been flirting with him. When she asked why he wasn't turning the pages of his book, he said it was hard reading. She laughed. She suggested he try moving his lips. He stared at the page. He closed his eyes and distress claimed its victory over him in the dark. The tray was removed, and he pretended to wake from his pretended sleep. The young woman asked if he believed this new invention, nondairy creamer, caused cancer. He said he had no experience in the matter. The young woman said he looked as if something was bothering him, his face was the color of nondairy creamer—no offense meant—and she hoped things would turn out all right. If it was about love, he would forget; and if someone had died, he would also forget. Of course, when people get sick, sometimes they stay sick for a while.

He thanked the young woman for her company.

He still felt his younger daughter's fingers on his shoes. His chest hurt.

He got home to San Francisco stunned and cold, and he had a blister on his lip, and he unplugged the telephone and crawled into bed. The winter fog had cleared. There was a thin sunlight on his window. He slept.

When he awakened, he called his mother to say, "I saw the girls, they're fine, they're growing, they asked about you."

"What did they ask?"

"They asked everything," he said. "What kids ask."

Eventually the former wife did not have another child. That scene seemed to have been cut from the script. She divorced the new husband anyway. The old husband did not remarry her. She did not frighten him again with pre-dawn telephone calls.

Eventually the daughters grew up.

A freshman in college, his elder daughter played her flute for a strike and parade to demonstrate against war, injustice, bureaucracy, anomie, and in favor of the solidarity of the student class. The university administration under siege, its men's rooms occupied by women, its supplies of copier paper cut off by radicals, its conscience stirred, decided upon a nuanced surrender as the most viable option. The strikers won most of their immediate demands, but the student dropped out of school anyway. How could the university be respected when it did piggish things, such as not granting all their nonnegotiable demands at once? And how could the university be respected when it also tried to give up its piggish ways so easily? What kind of character is that? What was there to learn in such an undefined place? Anyway, this was not the time for school, was it? In a world at war? With injustice and bureaucracy and loneliness everywhere?

She sought a place without piggishness and without power, without refined sugar and cultivated. World weary, she sought only to finish her nineteenth year in peace. It was hard to find perfection and the meaning of life when need pressed down so hard. How could a person escape junk food, sexism, and the ghosts of childhood? She found a commune in Mountain View, California.

The father did not approve. His approval, of course, was not part of the plan. He took counsel with his new wife and decided not to express anger; not to express enthusiasm, either; but to remain resolutely paternal and interested. In fact, he was pleased that she picked a refuge not far from his home. He asked the daughter to invite him to dinner at her commune and she did so. He brought wine and sourdough bread from the city, and his wife and their new baby, and his daughter cooked dinner for the visitors and for six or seven male communards who assured each other that wine was organic, an upper, and it caused the mind to expand. "Really," said one. "Besides mushrooms, it was the psychedelic of choice in Athenian times."

"Greek," said another, explaining history and geography to the visitors. "Greece, where they had mind-expanders even before Mexico. My parents always drink wine, too."

"They'll do that sometimes," said a fellow revolutionary. "But they just do it for kicks."

The visitors wondered why the one young woman in this egalitarian society cooked the meal. The new wife inquired.

"Hassles, we got to avoid hassles," said the expert on Athens and Greece. "Whatever's right we do."

"Everybody's got a thing," said another. "I got a thing, too."

"We discuss it openly," said the Athenian, carefully avoiding the word *rap*. "We lay it all out and, well . . ."

But if he couldn't say *rap*, what could he say?

"That's why this commune really works," said his friend. "Ever since we got over our hassle last Thursday it really works."

"Really," said the father.

Today was Saturday. The daughter wore an apron throughout dinner—a "ragout stew," one of the bilingual young men called it, plus a salad and the visitors' bread and wine. The commune worked, as the young man said, but the daughter *worked*. It was a tasty meal. The boiled onions in the stew were a special favorite of the father. At the end of the evening the daughter kissed her "wicked stepmother" with genuine fondness and the father's heart was lightened. The daughter would be okay. Someday she would listen fastidiously to Bob Dylan and not remember the names of these young men.

A few months later she left the commune, remarking, "Man, was I used," and went back to the university. "Someone as dumb as I am," she said, "I need an education."

"You're smart," her father told her.

"Tell me about your grandmother Hilda again. Didn't you tell me all the women in our family are not what any sane person would expect?"

"I'm not sure it's the genes. And it applies to the men, too."

"Goes without saying, dad. Why is everything so complicated?"

In 1973 this eldest daughter, still looking for a better way than the complication, was living on a kibbutz in Israel, teaching art and working in the fields. One morning in October a telephone call awakened her father in San Francisco. The boy in the room next to hers, a pilot, had been called before dawn to report to his base. Therefore she was one of the first to know the war had begun. She didn't tell him what it was, but she said, "Daddy, it's scary here."

The anguish in her voice was that of a grieving woman, not a girl.

He managed to get to Israel on the fifth day, as the names of the first casualties were announced. The country was in mourning and the nation was in an immense stir as the roar proceeded overhead and on the roadways, airplanes, rockets, armor, icy tracks in the sky and a deafening clatter on the ground. On the kibbutz those left behind were trying to get the harvest in. During a quiet moment, alone with his daughter, she showed him her calendar, where she had written: *Planted winter garden. Today war.*

They sat in a dining hall and she folded paper napkins as they talked. "Stop fidgeting," he said. "The napkins don't have to be folded."

She did not smile at this paternal nagging imported from America. "Everyone's tired. They deserve a neat table." Her concentration on the trivial folding of paper was a kind of mourning, and it had the lonely distance of mourning. And yet there was a sharp attention to the task which he remembered from *bougainvillea, lizard, donkey* on the Petionville road in Haiti.

At the end of the day, when the pilot from the room next

door called to say he was still alive, she wept in her father's arms.

As she traveled, like him in his travels, she left her personal belongings in transit—heart, soul, devotion, hopes, regrets. And he felt himself blessed in this daughter.

A year later, the daughter was still on the kibbutz, but the father was no longer living with his second wife. In the degrading of love, the distraction and racketing noise of a divorce, the vacant misery of inconsequence, longing for what he no longer had, he visited his eldest child. He flew to the place where he had gone to comfort her in the coming of war. Her winter garden was growing. She put her arms around him and said his trouble made her sad.

He clung to her. Then he lay like a baby in a hot afternoon, fretful and distraught on her bed, while she went out to work. She had her own life. He could draw family to him, but they had their own lives. This did not displease him; he felt eased. Surrounded by her few possessions, the pens and fuzzy-wuzzies and souvenirs of a woman who had made the difficult way safely out of girlhood—his own daughter!—he drifted down into sleep.

When she woke him for dinner, he said, "I'm glad to be here," and she said she was glad, too, and later he told her his troubles, repeating himself, as lovers do, and then he slept again. In her little room he felt like a child cared for by a mother.

"It's all reversed," he said. "This is what happens when a father gets old."

"This is temporary, dad. You're only old for a few minutes."

"A daughter becomes a mother."

"Not yet, dad," she said.

"No," he agreed, "not yet. But we have a little preview of coming attractions, don't we?"

6 My father grew old. He sat and waited in Cleveland. He slept and ate and sometimes trudged in the hall, past my brother's room, past my mother's room, past the laundry room, and then back to his room, or he could walk around the block if someone took him. He used to be entertained by his troubles. Now they gave him no pleasure.

"Dad!" I yelled across the long distance connection. "How are you?"

"What? What? Are you here?"

I was trying to poke through the shriveled nerves of his

96

ears. "No, no, dad, I'm in California, but I'm coming to see you soon."

"Are you far away?"

"I'm coming to see you soon!"

"You're far away."

And so I flew back to visit him and he touched me, he reached for my hand, he was nearly blind, he touched my face, he asked, "Are you here, son?"

"Of course I'm here, dad."

"No, son, you're far away. I'm far away."

I smelled the old man, the staleness, the medicines on his breath; I saw the clothes which hadn't changed in years—no need for new clothes. He used to be a natty dresser. A few years ago one of my sons sat on his lap and pulled the button off this shirt; my mother sewed a different button on it. "Dad," I said, "let's go for a walk."

This topcoat. This hat with the jaunty feather. A few years ago he took my sons for bus rides on his knees; before that, he bounced me in the same way, hup, hup, hup!

We took tiny steps on the sidewalk outside his apartment building and he said, "I don't want to go to a home. Sometimes I think I better go to a home. I can't take care of myself."

"You're still you, dad."

"I don't think I'm going to get any better. Mother keeps asking me if I'm going to get any better. I don't know what the doctors tell her. I don't think so."

"Are they treating you okay around here?"

"What? What?"

"Are they treating you okay, dad?"

"It would be better if you was here. I feel better when you're here. They don't dare get mean to me when you're around, son."

"Dad, they're not mean to you."

Silence. Cars whooshing up the slope toward Shaker Square. A lawnmower. I was watching the cracks in the sidewalk and his small feet in black slip-on shoes with elastic tops. It was hard for me to walk so slowly. He stopped and turned with his hand on my arm. He said, "I can't stick up for myself so good anymore. I used to be able to yell. I didn't need to hit since the Depression, that business was rough, but people knew I could hit. I can't see, I can't hear, I can't taste. . . ."

"You were very strong, dad. I remember how you carried a hammer in your back pocket and nobody bothered you."

"I'm tired, let's go home, I'm dizzy, I need to lay down."

"Back so soon?" my mother asked. "It's a nice day outside. Get some exercise, you'll eat better, Sam. I made pot roast today and I don't want you wasting."

I tucked him into his bed. "Help me turn over," he said. He could turn himself over, but he liked to be touched, he could feel the hands.

Five minutes later he appeared in his shorts and undershirt and said, "You're still here."

"Of course, dad."

"Let's just walk down the hall. I can't sleep. Are you hungry?"

"No, dad. Are you?"

"Well, if you're hungry, I'll eat a little Jell-O with you. Can you heat the milk?"

"I can do that, dad."

I thought he was smiling. He said, "You're learning. I wish you didn't go far away, son."

"Well, I'm here," I said. "Let's not think about far away."

"Nobody eats now!" my mother said. "I made a good dinner."

"What time is it?" my father asked. "In a few days you'll be gone again. And then who knows when I'll see you?"

My father was tired of growing old. He wished me to fix this for him. He used to fix things for me. He helped me grow up. Why couldn't I help him now?

Sometimes he made a mess. "I did it," he said. "I did it."

"Accidents happen, dad. Anyone can make a mistake."

"I did it, son. I didn't used to do that. Don't tell me anyone can do it. I did it."

"It's all right, dad."

"It's not all right. I don't want to do that. I shouldn't do that. How come I let myself do that, son?"

We sat in the room with his special chair, with his lamp with the magnifying lens that he didn't use for reading because he couldn't read anymore, nothing seemed to magnify print large enough, bright enough; he couldn't work the machine, the arm and swivel over the neckrest, it was too complicated; he rested his head, white face, white eyes, white hair, against the black vinyl; he asked, "Are you still here, son?"

"Of course I'm here, dad."

"You want to go out someplace? You want to have fun?"

"I'm all right, dad. I'm staying with you."

"You should go out, son. Don't leave me."

My mother had a meeting. It was good for her. How else could she survive? The girls—that's what she called them— had projects, the hospital, the welfare federation, the bond drive, but tonight there was a little game. My brother and I were supposed to make dinner for our father. My brother squinted at me and said, "Dad likes delicatessen."

"Dad?" I asked. "You want to go out for dinner?"

"Mother doesn't like me to go out. She left food in the box. She said there's food in the oven."

"Dad, it'll keep. Why don't we go to Sharpie's?"

"Sharpie's?" He grinned. "Is that good for me?"

"I wouldn't worry about that," I said.

"You can eat good things, mushroom barley soup, a sandwich, pastrami," my brother said. "I'll cut the fat off."

"I can't worry about that," he said.

We helped him dress. He asked, "Where's my hat?"

"It's warm out, dad."

"Where's my hat?"

My brother drove and told him what we were seeing, where we were going. Our father answered that he knew where we were going, and he named the streets, he seemed to see the houses. He knew what was out there. He saw shadows, lights and darks, he knew. He said, "Now turn into this parking lot, it's a shortcut, now you're at Sharpie's."

"That's right, dad," my brother said. I could see that my brother was happy. He too wanted to eat out, mushroom barley soup, baskets of good bread, wet coleslaw, spicy meats, cheesecake.

The delicatessen was crowded. They had expanded it since I was last on the premises. In honor of the Cleveland Indians there were Indian clubs on the walls. The framed mirrors made the place look even larger and people could watch themselves eat if they were so inclined. The extra floor space made room for the many non-Jews who also have developed cravings for corned beef. "Jewish soul food," I said.

"What?" asked my dad.

My brother was shaking his head. Impossible to get

through with an explanation now. In the dead of night, when he waked and called to be turned over, or wandered the hallway in search of a snack, he could sometimes hear and follow whole sentences, he liked to ask questions or tell stories, he could talk and listen. But now we had to talk like Indians—minimal communication, stone faces.

I was not an Indian, nor was my father. I said, "It's good for lots of people, dad. Everyone comes to eat here now. The goyim have picked up on corned beef, pastrami, bagels and lox."

"It's bigger," he said. "It's noisy. Was it always so noisy?"

His hearing aid was shrieking. He fiddled anxiously with the dial. It must hurt the dead nerves which are not quite dead. He snapped something; perhaps he was turning it off entirely. My brother said, "He can't hear when it's noisy like this."

Plates were clattering. Children were yelling. The waiters were running. It was Sunday night. People were shouting at friends. It was a family night. In Cleveland they don't eat out so often, but on Sunday night they eat out at Sharpie's. The loudspeaker was calling names. Table for two for Bernstein. Party of four, Malinsky. Dr. Epstein, will you kindly call your service?

"When can we sit down?" my father asked. "I usually eat at six."

"You can wait, dad," I said. "It won't hurt you."

"I have to take my medicine at six-thirty, after dinner. When can we sit down?"

My brother said, "Here's the lady, she'll show us our table."

It was Mrs. Sharpie and she said, "Sam, Sam! How are you?"

101

"Fine, fine, fine, fine. Everything been going fine," he said.

"This is a nice table, Sam?" she asked.

"Fine, fine, fine, you too," he said. "And the husband, the kids. I hope the same for them."

The codgers who used to lag behind him, poorer, dumber, less renowned and respected, even less healthy, now they were ahead of him. They had the jump on him at last. They were here scarfing down delicatessen—yelling, laughing, greeting, gossiping, judging the textures and perfume of smoked fish, chomping pickles, enjoying the chaotic eating all around them, digesting or doing their best. The codgers ran up to grab my father's hand and say, "Sam! Sam! Where you been? You look great, Sam!"

"Over here, Sam! Look over here! It's Jake, Jacob!"

"Hullo," he said, "fine, good to see you, fine, fine, fine, fine."

"They haven't seen him in a while," my brother explained. "They thought maybe he was dead. The ones who were jealous of him hoped he was senile. He knows. He's glad to be out."

We sat and he spread the menu in front of him and studied it through the milky blue-white eyes. After he finished running down the menu with his fingers, touching the glaze, feeling the tassel, pretending to read, he turned toward me and said, "You order, son. You know what I like."

"Dad!" called my brother. "The mushroom barley soup?"

"You order for me, boys," he said. "I feel kind of hungry today. I feel kind of good. Is this Sunday?"

"Of course, dad. Everybody's at Sharpie's."

"I knew," he said with satisfaction. "Where are the breadsticks? The salty ones, please. Give me some butter, too. I can do it. Give me the knife, please, son."

My brother tucked the napkin under his collar. I said, "No, don't do that, let him spill it if he wants to," and my brother said, "I live here, you don't, he doesn't need to spill the soup on his shirt."

My brother was right.

While he ate, the codgers kept running up to the table, shaking his hand, crying out their identifications, Jake! Morris! Murray and Danny, Al the printer's sons! Nice to see you, Sam. Good you're out again! Thought you was sick, Sam, but you look great! You gonna start doing the deli again Sundays, Sam?

"Fine, fine, fine, fine," he said.

When we left, threading ourselves like a holy progression through the eaters and celebrants, my father bowed graciously in the direction of the praise and obeisance aimed at him, smiling, the milky eyes squeezed in smiles, seeing and hearing the praise somehow, his cheeks less gray, pink showing under the flat white bristles, blushing as he turned his head this way and that.

In the car, when the noise was gone, he switched his hearing aid up again.

"You seemed to hear them without your machine," I said.

"Yes, yep, seemed like that," he said. "So much noise. I hear too much. It hurts the ears."

"Dad, is it okay now?"

"Sure I can. Always can. Fine, son."

"Dad, who were all those men?"

"What?"

"Who were all those people in Sharpie's, dad?"

He grinned and looked at me. He looked in my direction, he looked hilariously into my eyes and seemed to see me.

103

He was laughing and laughing and holding my hand on the back seat of the car while my brother drove. It was a marvelous joke to him. "You think I remember?" he asked. "You think I know?"

The next day I caught a flight to San Francisco. I had work to do. I missed my children.

"You'll come back soon? You'll call? But I can't talk on the phone so good. When will you come back? Next week? Soon? Tomorrow?"

"Fine, fine, fine, fine," I said.

"No," he said. "Not good."

He sat in his chair under the magnifying glass and the intense light he no longer used for reading, enjoying the heat perhaps, and looked stiff and stony, unblinking in the light, like a statue.

He seemed to know something.

Neither he nor I understood what it was. Just then, how should I know? But someday we'll both find out.

7 WHEN I arrived one day in Cleveland, surprising my family, my mother was bathing, powdering, dressing, and putting on her wig. She powdered with Johnson's like a furious athlete for her date that night; a white cloud floated out of her bedroom. My father was sitting in his chair with the magnifying glass lifted like a visor above his head and the powerful light for reading unlit. He was staring straight ahead. His hands rested on the arms of the chair. No portrait was being snapped. Some of mother's bustle was to replace the noise he used to make.

She had a fail-safe plan whenever I dropped out of the skies without notice. "Are you hungry?" she asked.

"I just wanted to see you all." I sneezed. An attack of Johnson's Baby Powder.

"Are you hungry?"

"No, you're going out. I can take something if I'm hungry. Have a good time, I'll stay with dad."

"Just a second, here, you're home, I have to go down to the store," she said.

"There's plenty to eat. Never mind. What are you going for?"

"I'll make you a can of piping hot vegetable soup. I'll be right back."

"But you've got plenty here!" I opened a cabinet. There were serried ranks of soup, vegetable, tomato, tomato-beef, beef-tomato, chicken, chicken rice, chicken chunks, chicken broth, chicken-turkey—"The pantry's full of soup! Look! Heinz! Campbell! Manischewitz! Rokeach! And those ones with the labels washed off you got for a bargain!"

"I think that's S & W," she said. "A flood in the basement of the Cedar superette."

"So you got soup, mother."

She gazed patiently at one spot or another in the air near my head. "You're company from far-off places. Don't I know how to treat company? I want to get you a fresh can." She looked shrewd. "Wait, just wait. Your children will laugh at you, too."

"Mother, they do already—"

"Don't reprehend me," she said. "I can climb the highest mountain, like the title song from the movie I heard on the radio, unless it's a stick shift. I kind of like that fluid drive automatic. And that's what I'm getting ready for Israel bonds tonight—climb the highest mountain to get money from the lowest of the low."

She was smiling with the incomprehensible hilarity of

her older sister, Anna. The sisters had learned it from their mother, Hilda. She was sad and she was smiling. She had also learned sadness from her mother. She knew I was grown far away from her. Why this smile which said not to pity her? Why this smile which asked me not to tease her about soup, about habits, about what she was and life is? She smiled because that was her way. Smiles made a nicer curve around troubles.

Hilarity was a weapon of the women in this family.

"Where are you going to climb the highest mountain today?"

"I'm crazy so mad at him."

"He can't help it, mother, he—"

My father in his chair seemed to hear her. His arms jerked and then settled back on the chair. Sometimes the Parkinsonism fought through the L-Dopa and the twitches seized him, and then the drug took charge again and he subsided.

"Not you, dad!" I called. "Everything's all right!"

"Fine, fine, fine, fine," he said. "I hope so."

She explained that it was another who had roused her ire and the itch of business. Al Polasky. Why Al, the paper man, the box manufacturer, almost as old as dad? Because he wouldn't buy his quota of Israel bonds. "It would be better he should buy," she said, gritting her teeth, "better for him. He's a pickanoonie."

"Picayune, mother?"

"You heard me—very small. He thinks he's cute, but not very big. I don't suppose he wants an outstanding personality because he don't got one. Totally pickanoonie about everything, including he doesn't give to charity more than anybody else doesn't give around here. He's the only one, the worst. Who's he going to leave it to? His children got plenty."

I wanted to ask what she could do, but it seemed, as she finished outfitting herself in Halle Bros. best—noisy fabrics, a strong seduction and persuasion outfit for a pickanoonie—she had a plan. "I'm taking him for a drive," she said.

"Where?"

"A funeral. To his own funeral. Old man can't breathe without rattling the woodwork. I'm taking him to the nice cemetery out there on Mayfield. This is where you'll be if you don't give, I tell him. I know what he says: I'll get there anyway. Then I go, So smart, you might as well buy. And I stand there and the wind from the dead blows on us and he says why did I come for a ride with you, Frieda? You give me a whiff of the end. And I say because, because I happened to ask you, and he says, But we're old folks now, and I say, *You* are. I'm just a salelady for bonds for Israel. And then I wait. I got lots of time. Your father ain't going noplace. I wait."

"When you coming home, Frieda?" my father asked, looking straight ahead from his chair.

"When I'm finished with Al Polasky."

"When you come home, Frieda?" my father asked.

My mother said to me in a low voice, "You see?"

"I'll stay with dad," I said.

She finished her fortifications and decorations while I sat on the edge of the bed and promised to take food from the box if I got hungry, but not to spoil my appetite. I watched the dressing. Garments, supports, concealments, straps, buckles, zippers. And then hair.

"Mother," I said, "your own hair is better."

She knew what was coming. She fixed her lips. "It's thin," she said. "It's whiskey."

"Mother, it's your own hair. You know how I hate these wigs."

"How can you hate so much? What's the hate? Why are you such a hater? Who raised you to give spite on me looking nice? In the hair department, my wig is Genuine Non-Korn Sunburst Glory."

"Noncorn, mother?"

"Not one of those cheapie Korn wigs from Kornea."

"Korean, mother. Non-Korean."

"That's what I told you. One of those places they cut the hair out in bunches to sell to baldies like me. Not so far as baldies, but whiskeys. So I got this real hair wig like I got to cover my whiskey hair. This is a real hair wig and it's all mine."

"How can a wig be all your own?"

"Didn't I pay for it with my husband's hard-earned money? I don't buy things on time like some of those ethnic neighborhoods, they know who I mean. No one in our family ever heard from prepossessing for didn't payment. This is my own Genuine Non-Korn Sunburst Glory hair. I got to cover my whisks when I go out with the girls and their silver tresses, don't I? They're really happy for me even if they get a little jealous. It's different. They don't all have old husbands can afford Sunburst Glory hair without blinking an eye. Course, he don't blink his eyes enough anymore. They all dry out. I got to see he takes his drops."

Her Medicare and Social Security canasta-playing girl-friends, some of them, had income from their very good providers, their often dead husbands, sometimes not dead yet. They believed in staying pretty at seventy-five or eighty. They were happy for each other. Even at the funer-

109

als, they were happy for good health. God bless everyone, dead or alive, with a few exceptions. He, praise his name, should take care of the men, too, since the doctors aren't much help. Sophie, for example, preferred a little drink to help her good nature keep on rolling along, Courvoisier in Diet Seven-Up, but never more than three per evening— maybe just one more for a nightcap. She was the only shicker in the group, probably too many troubles, children scattered and don't write too often. She only got quiet under the potion. A little alcohol rubdown on the brain and the broken heart. My mother thought all that Diet Seven-Up wasn't good for her. She should vary it with a ginger ale— give the stomach a rest. Nice sweet Vernor's imported from Detroit. Some of the other girls—Sophie, too, of course, it went with the drinking—smoked. Smoked cigarettes. But they all used filters. They weren't looking for trouble. And all of them ate. And also some of them were so old they were finally getting their fondest wish. It came true. Nice and slim. No matter how much they ate, they could eat to their heart's content and still lose weight. Finally, at eighty, they were getting svelte and lovely, like the blondies some of their husbands used to run around with on business trips in the old days that would never come back anymore.

This last slimming, everybody claps hands and, a little bit jealous, unfortunately often leads to breaking a hip or a little touch of cancer and another funeral. "She looked so good." "Still does, but now she's dead." "Well, that's life. Same thing happens to so many people in our city of Cleveland."

Mother was not svelte; she was still solid. This afternoon there was a stirring of chiffon and a tucking of braces and belts and a patting with the palm of the hand, not the fingers, of the wig; a little tug here and there with the fingers. Nothing more to be said. Another empty chair at the canasta table. Vernor's ginger ale for everyone in honor of Bessie. A little Courvoisier in a certain person's glass.

"How can you drink that strong brown stuff from the old country?"

"In France, everybody drinks it. They take it after dinner, like for heartburn."

"Here, in this country, we got modern medicines, Tums for the tummy, Alka-Spritzer, we don't have to take that old country stuff. It burns when you smell it."

"In France they sniff it first, then they swallow."

"No wonder they're like that in France. Oh, that smell. Quick, put some ginger ale in it."

She was supposed to be on her way to deal with Al Polasky, but with her son home like this, a surprise, probably very hungry from that terrible airplane cooking, she didn't know if she should trust me to heat a fresh can of soup, eat something nice. There were sons and there were bonds and a mother's work could never be undone.

Al Polasky didn't have a missus anymore. My mother was steaming at him. Polasky was an unlucky old kid. She intended to drive him to the graveyard and show him where he was headed whether or not he bought bonds, it was immaterial in any case, but she also wanted to dress nicely to steam at him. She intended to look her Sunburst Glory best while she was causing him sweat and nervousness and his teeth would go sliding around on his gums. She was flirtatious and furious. "When I get home," she said winsomely, "now you're here, I want to take you downstairs to the storeroom."

"I don't think I need anything, mother."

"Need, need, you *want*, don't you? Are you an American person?"

"Let's talk when you get home. Have a successful mission."

"I'll bomb him out," she said, "I'll aggravate him till he'll rue the day he's gonna die. Personally, I'm an American girl with justice on my side."

"I'll be fine with dad. Take your time. I'll just sit here with him."

"How many years can he just sit? When's he going to get better? He's not his old self anymore."

"Frieda?" my father asked. "Are you talking about me?"

"What's to say?" she asked. "Why should I talk?"

"I can't hear," he said. "Is it time for my four o'clock pills?"

"We'll tell you. Pills. They don't do any good. *Sam! Someone will tell you!* He doesn't hear me," she said. "What can I do? He won't listen."

Often when my mother thought I was tiring of sitting with my father, and also had eaten enough, and might be in danger of going out for a walk with my brother, slipping out of the family onto the streets filled with pool tables, fast drivers, muggers, germs, she retrieved her ace in the hole, what Sid called "Mother's Blue Chip Redemption Center." This was the room in which she kept her treasures obtained from Blue Chip stamps, Eagle stamps, and opening savings accounts in neighborhood banks all over the fair city of Cleveland. Folding umbrellas, electric can openers, Teflon pans, off-brand mixers, hot combs, pen-and-pencil sets. "Do you want to go downstairs and take something home with you?" she asked. Corningware, un-Sanyo calculators, non-Cartier digital watches, anti-Sony portable radios, batteries not included.

"I already have five umbrellas from the last time," I said.

"How about a Jiffy Hamburger Grill? You got already in your house an electric knife?"

"I don't do that much carving, mother."

"When you have the kids over for Thanksgiving dinner?"

"Mother, I seem to eat other people's Thanksgiving dinner. I take cakes or wine as my contribution."

"You need some cake pans, son?"

"I'll have a shower now."

It turned out, this week only, she had a special fine-spray shower nozzle in the Redemption Museum, a once-in-a-lifetime item. It came from the Slovenian Savings & Loan of Parma.

In ten minutes a miracle occurred. Instead of running out to take Al Polasky to his preview of coming attractions funeral, she gathered my brothers and our father for dinner. After dinner she would go. She telephoned. Al understood. Al could wait. Four-thirty in the afternoon is a little early for dinner, but this was a special occasion. I thought and thought and thought in a long hot flash of world-historical self-criticism, and considered some more, and then decided to eat. I would say nothing. I would say nothing. I would say nothing.

It's so easy to give pleasure. All you have to do is open the mouth—a well-known fact and item.

"Well, the family mostly together again, except your father doesn't listen or talk," she said. "This was just something I whipped up in a jiffy."

My brothers and I ate. Our middle-aged heads bent to our plates. Our father used a wide spoon. We were together again. Mother served.

"Have some of my nice salad."

One, I thought. "Thank you, later," I said.

113.

"Have my nice salad."

Two, I thought. "My plate is full," I said.

"Are you dating anybody special?" she asked. "I made this salad for you."

Three, I thought. My brother Sid moved somnambulistically toward iceberg lettuce. The call of carrot bewitched him.

"Here, I'll put the salad in your plate for you—the fresh green pepper will fit right here next to the potato."

I pushed her hand back toward its arm, shoulder, and socket. I performed this response heavily, a tidal undersea gesture, nature and instinct recalled, meaning no harm. *Four*, I thought.

"But you're not eating my salad?" she asked.

"Five," I said aloud.

"What's that five?"

"Five times you offered me the salad."

"That's all? What kind of hostess and mother only offered five times? We're having dinner. It's got vitamins you like, roughage which is good for you—maybe you want just the tomatoes, cucumbers, lettuce, a radish at least, hold you while I handle Al Polasky a few hours, I'll forget about the fresh garden green peppers?" she inquired with gentle hope. I didn't answer and something ungreen, unsalad in the air warned her to change the subject. She said, "Divorced fathers on the march."

"What?"

"Did you read in the paper divorced fathers on the march? They say it's one of those nice little revolutions we're having so much nowadays. In my day they didn't, did you ever?"

"Did I ever what?"

"Did you ever look up your cousin Don? He's a divorced

father too, you have a lot in common. I'm putting the salad away now."

"Six," I said.

"That doesn't count," she said. "I was only stating facts. Divorced father, so you're not marching? You'll have it for dinner. Don't get your roughage now, get it later. This was late lunch. Did your friend Shapiro ever remarry a nice girl this time? He looks so lacks a daisical, but he got a good daisical for his profession. I hear he's highly respected. None of you boys are mental patients like some people. But a nice wife wants a doer around the house." She gazed at the bowl of salad about which she had announced putting-away intentions and plucked a piece of celery which happened to stick out. She evened out the ensemble. "If you ask me," she said, "the book was better'n the movie."

"What book?"

"Didn't I tell you about that movie I saw with the girls? They put in a lot of sex stuff to fool the people. It reminded me of your friend. Dusty Allen lacks a daisical in that one, too."

"Dustin Hoffman? Woody Allen?"

"Naturally, he's terrific in his office, whatever he does. And I'll bet his mother don't make a salad for him and he forgets to take a bite."

"His mother died thirty years ago, mother."

"Poor boy. No wonder. Did he get over it yet? How can anybody blame him? Why you got that brown scorch stain on your shirt?"

The brown scorch stain offered a chance to introduce the larger changing world of today to the dinner table. "Your average nineteen-year-old girlfriend who insists on ironing your shirt to show her love'll do that sometimes, mom."

"Sha! Don't talk dirty! This is not a movie who you got

to impress? And no nice little tee shirt underneath to protect the chest in the damp, is that how she dresses you? In a telltale brown scorch stain? All you divorced boys, Don, your other friend Shapiro, all your buddies I used to feed when they were kids, no one tells them about wash-n-wear anymore? You can hang it up in the bathroom overnight and presto?"

"No, mother."

"So don't you discuss with your friends? You just eat junky food and nineteen-year-old girls you date? Feh, my son."

I sighed. "Mother, she's twenty-nine. Sometimes you make me want to tease you."

"Lying I call it. I've had more experience than you, I don't care your education. If twenty-nine, why not thirty-nine? Why not thirty-nine ninety-five, a special? So why you teasing? And if you don't get the roughage, sure as shootin', you'll strain. You'll strain, my son."

Wings whirred in her head when she contemplated her offspring and her husband. Propellers stirred, and then wings vibrated in the wind. She feared our enemies. She tried to name them with words, which were not her gift except in quantity. She used words to weaken enemies, attract benefits, cover the known world with nice and with discipline. Is Hitler gone forever? Does Don, does Tom still talk about her cookies? What about their children—are they smart like yours? What does life mean? Answer this question, son.

For many years I had been a son to my mother, oppositional, straining. Now grown out of her easy sight, a parent myself, I was engaged in matters for which other sorts of attention were required. Yet with her, in her presence and sometimes even in her absence, I still consented to validate

116

my will by discussing the salad, the meat, and loves which were properly separated from her.

Like my mother, I seemed never to give up wanting happiness in love. And so of course I have been kept busy. I too make a mouth of my eyes. Take; eat.

Pay attention, I thought. This lady has also grown a little older.

Only history is a sure winner. My mother and father living after me in my children and grandchildren—that's a thing to count on.

"Now I got to go out and deal with that no-charity Al Polasky. I'll show him where he's going, sure as shootin', Al is on his way."

"You're powerful, mother."

"Thank you very much." She fielded my admiration gracefully. She also didn't let it distract her. "Now try to tell me why got a new divorce this time. I liked this wife," she said.

"So did I," I said.

"Well, maybe she'll wake up."

"No, it's not a dream. This we're doing wide awake."

"Well, well," she said. "You got nice babies. That's a plus-and-a-half. And you're still young. Why are you smiling?"

I was old enough to be a grandfather. And I wasn't smiling.

"Come on, got to go now. While I'm gone, I made some bran muffins and strawberry jam. You always like bran muffins and strawberry jam, son."

It was true I liked that wife. But there was nothing my mother could do for my marriage unless I let go and wept, and for her I was not doing that. I didn't save tears for her in my trophy room. So she fell into the giving of food.

When she fell into silence, her rare silence, it was a form of understanding and kindness, prayer, a boisterous song of silence. When she fell into food, it was my fault, or my brothers' or father's, and it could be remedied by obedience to cooking. When she gave both food and silence, it was a mixture of love and reproach and, I think, even tenderness.

"When I come home from Al Polasky," she said, "we'll talk."

She took the old miser out for a drive. It was one of her little moves, one of her tricks. To the Mayfield Cemetery. And then she told where he could end. Right there. In the dark. Soon. And then she asked certain questions. And she made certain statements. And she waited for a reply.

He signed the pledge card and told her she was terrific, Frieda.

I know, she said. Plus I knew you would.

She was tired from all the driving when she returned. Now that my father was so tired all the time, my mother was keeping busy with selling bonds for Israel, with the girls and their games, with current events and the good books. "I'm learning to move my lips when I'm reading," she said, "really get my teeth into it. I read someplace how everybody got to go someday. I read how you can't take it with you. You read how Al Polasky gonna buy bonds on a regular schedule?"

"I didn't read that, mother."

"That's because I'm just writing it up in my book." A smile of enraged glee played over her face. Her own mother, Hilda, was able to manage difficult men, too. She removed her Sunburst Glory wig. On her knees she had smears of cemetery mud where she had knelt to show Al

Polasky where he was headed. In her pocketbook she had a check for a bond.

8 PINK TURNS gray, plump turns pinched, everyone moves on. Aunt Anna had always been my mother's link with Hilda and the country of the past, her guide, her big sister. The big sister shrank, the passing of years drying out the life still concentrated and focused within. She grew very old. But escaping the common rules, she also moved into a green delight in survival. She refused to be an ordinary miracle and emblem. The hilarity hard times had held back was released. Ancient now, nothing could threaten her, nothing more could stop her, each day was a sly victory. There was power in a survival which carried this tiny bent person beyond regret, beyond mourning, beyond desire, into some pure arena where nothing can hurt; there is no hurt or healing that matters at the end; and yet the past continued, today was still vivid, and she took strength from the air, emitting steady comment. The offering of advice might be a family trait as permanent as dust and bones.

When I last saw her, Aunt Anna was ninety-six or maybe only ninety-five years old and asked to be reminded: "How many children you got, Herbert?"

"Five."

"You married?"

"Not now."

"Herbert! Did you say five? Are you going to have any more children?"

I held her hand and looked into the milky, tensely squinting eyes. The hand was hard, dry, small, and firm, and it gripped back. The hair was thin. The attention was complete.

"Herbert! You deaf? I told you: you having any more kids?"

"I won't if you won't, Aunt Anna," I said. She held both my hands to keep from falling as laughter vibrated through the wires and filaments of her body. Her children—a retired doctor, a retired lawyer, a retired teacher, a retired businessman, a widow—pushed around her.

"I'm only laughing and choking a little," she said. "Go away. Leave me alone to laugh with this boy."

My mother, who was eighty-two or so, talked with her every day on the telephone. They exchanged the gossip of family—births, deaths, marriages, quarrels, wills, children, children, children unto the third or fourth generation, spreading out from Cleveland and beyond, ripples on a gigantic pool. They complained about the problems of other people's aging, not their own.

Aunt Anna's children worried about her living alone. But she refused to move in with one of them or (out of the question, you crazy?) into a "home." When they hired someone to stay with her, she told the woman to go, she fired her. "Who do I need a cleaning? What do I need a cleaning? I did all my life for other people, I can't do for myself?"

"Be reasonable, ma."

"That's a good idea. All at once everybody in the whole world be that."

Someone in the family went to the market and visited her daily. She consented to these attentions. Even if nobody in the whole world was that, she would be reasonable. "Don't forget to buy the family-size oatmeal."

"I know about shopping," said the widow.

"You could make a mistake," said Aunt Anna.

"So *once* I got the large and not the family."

"That's what we got to avoid. That's why I say I can do my shopping. Mistakes make a person cranky."

"Ma, I'll be careful."

She didn't want to nag a poor old widow, her daughter. Her teeth clacked shut. Her blind eyes glistened with desire to do her own shopping.

"I want my independence," she said. "At ninety-four, I can't do what I want yet? I still got to watch out for other people?"

"You said you were ninety-five, ma," the retired lawyer said.

"So you tell me. I know different. I don't feel ninety-five yet."

"You don't look it—does she?" the retired teacher asked.

"A family consultation," she remarked. "First kids wet on my shoulder and then they argue their own mother is too old. But they retired. I didn't retire. Too old for what? I can still do my floors—what can they do?"

She had always been small; she shrank as if time were a zinc tub and she was wool and washed in hot water. The family worried about her nourishment. At a wedding at the Oakwood Club for the daughter of a niece, we sat gathered at one large table. My mother and Aunt Anna were shouting the news together. The retired children urged her to eat. I returned from the buffet with a plate of scallops and Aunt Anna found them, began to pluck them up and chew and swallow, one after the other. She sighed. Her fork got busy. She had never eaten shellfish in her life, but this was the sort of country club where the Jews ate shellfish on weekends or special occasions. Her fork flew like the needle on a treadle-operated sewing machine.

Her children watched, in a dilemma akin to horror. They worried about her eating. They worried about her calcium, protein, carbohydrates. They liked to see her doing justice to her plate. They begged her to eat as, many years ago, she had begged them to eat. But they also knew she would die if she learned she was eating shellfish.

She finished the plate of soft, squirmy, sweetish, non-kosher flesh.

She turned to my mother, scraping her fork around and finding none left on the dish. She said, "Frieda! You like to get me some more of those nice noodles?"

An immediate high-level family treaty resolved the matter. Emergency situations and proper nutrition required a special deal with the Law. The children would be bringing cooked scallops to her house daily now. Rules were made for people. A retired lawyer said, "Those nice noodles, they're so slippery, why not use a spoon, ma?"

Aunt Anna's husband, not a great success in life, had died

years ago. Before he checked out she was to be pitied, rais-
ing a numerous family with a husband who seemed like one
of the children, only more boastful. During the Depression,
my parents carried baskets of food to them. The back seat
of the Pontiac smelled all week of leafy vegetables, bread,
and the east-side spiciness of salami. Mother believed in
filling the food baskets. Her family didn't believe in Relief;
the less contact with the state, the better. Aunt Anna's
husband went out for a walk while the baskets were unload-
ed. My father and mother carried; nobody helped. Along
with the food, filling the car each Sunday, came my brother
and me. Sometimes we slept over at Aunt Anna's house.
She wouldn't let us play with matches. She wouldn't let us
set the garage afire. Over whatever mysteries lay within,
she wore thick glasses, thin hair, and a continual smile. I
wondered what she was smiling about. The smile flickered
and played without reason--an American habit she brought
with her from Russia. I didn't resent too much not being
allowed to burn things, not even the garage, because her
oatmeal cookies were refreshing after my mother's oatmeal
cookies. I liked the dates she used instead of raisins. Maybe
the dates made her smile, and my liking her cookies more
than my mother's made her smile more. The sisters sometimes debated dates versus raisins, but it never came to a
serious break.

A few years earlier my grandfather had lived with Aunt
Anna. White-bearded, said to be a rabbi, he spoke almost no
English. He had never worked in America. I thought the
word "white" about his beard, but I knew he came from afar
and it was snowfrost in his beard which made the white-
ness. In America he played chess in the synagogue with the
other nonrabbis. He had no use for English or work. Toward the end of his nonrabbinical career he gave up chess

for checkers; he had no more use for chess. When we played, I liked the part where I kinged him, also the jumping and skipping two jumps part. Although he smiled through the snowfrost during our checker contests, he liked best, at this stage of his life, to pee outside in the yard. He loved the dense green fields of the Ukraine and, very old now, began to think that's where he was. He had a use for those fields.

Nevertheless, he understood that I was four years old, needing cookies along with the checkers, and he conspired with me to steal them between meals, during the few hours when no eating was supposed to be going on while the world prepared for later eating.

After stolen cookies he took me into the backyard for a healthful stroll and natural activity in the Ukraine.

Aunt Anna came out to find us and bring us inside for our naps. Since we had already eaten our cookies, we had no right to more; but since they were good for us, especially the dates, which not everyone fully understood, we were allowed another two or three with our warm milk. She couldn't afford Ovaltine, due to hard times, but plain milk did the job. The milk should not boil. She touched it with her wrist to make sure it was the right temperature—kids and old men had wristlike throats.

Sometimes, if we didn't stay overnight while my parents took some vacation from their noisome sons, we drove home through Cleveland after the last Sunday meal and my brother and I fell asleep on the back seat of the Pontiac to the visual rhythm of streetlamps and telephone wires, streetlamps, wires, until we were carried up to bed. My mother, Aunt Anna's baby sister, listened respectfully to her advice about childrearing. My brother and I fought her Ukrainian scientific theories about enemas, feeding, and winter clothing, although we gradually gave up lighting fires with kitchen matches. What convinced us? Maybe other games to play. We formed a united all-American front.

When Aunt Anna's children went off to Ohio State University to prepare for their various careers, they kept loyal contact with Cleveland, the fount of family. They sent the laundry home by mail. In return they received, along with clean shirts and underwear, mason jars of stewed prunes. A child can get constipated on that school food far from home. Sometimes, alas, the jar broke in transit, although carefully wrapped in clean laundry. Sticky and tensely straining mornings were the result. Aunt Anna was not discouraged by the malice and stupidity of Cossacks or postal employees, and the proof of her wisdom was that almost everyone turned out to have active careers and healthy stomachs, if you didn't count a few ulcers, acid conditions, cases of colitis, chronic constipation, diverticulitis, and those generalized gas problems which were the inevitable reward of mind-stretching professional work. (The liberal professions are known refuges for flatulence.)

When her father the nonrabbi died, it was a little like the future death of her husband. More room in the house for the children, more time for them, more cookies, dates, prunes, and a workshop for mending the socks and taking out hems. Aunt Anna cared for men without requiring them. Her smile predated men and it would survive them. That observant, certain smile which flickered over her lips.

As I grew older I still studied the rhythm of the streetlamps, but didn't sleep on the long drive from the east side to the west side. I noticed Aunt Anna's children becoming successful, heavier, married, and the family expanding mightily, exponentially, as the children begat children. I left Cleveland. On visits I saw Aunt Anna unchanging while her children and grandchildren were transformed. She already had bald grandsons. She still lived alone, cooked, baked, darned, and talked on the telephone.

"Frieda!" she said to my mother. "Your boys go out on any good dates or just those funny-funnies? Where's all the daughters you promised me?"

"Daughter-in-laws," my mother said.

"Where are they? I want more. I want wives for your boys like I got for mine. In the old country we fixed up these things—trouble with other things—no trouble these things—"

"I'll try," my mother said.

"Of course they're not nothing but pleasure. I remember a girl in our village, sweet wouldn't melt in her mouth, she did such things—"

One of her sons gave her a tape recorder and asked her to dictate the story of her life for an oral history project.

"You still talking to the Sonny?" my mother asked.

"A Victor I'll talk to, a Morris, even God forbid a Sheldon, but a Sonny? What I got to say to such a machine isn't even a person?"

Nevertheless, she talked for hours and hours about the past, poverty, migrations, trials, ultimate triumph, but found greater pleasure in telephoning my mother to discuss the events of the day, the present, what she willed for the future, that unpast full of promise. Someone was eating good. Someone was not. Someone had a good job. Someone was getting a better one. Someone was pregnant. When would someone else wake up and stop doing whatever he or she was doing and shouldn't do?

When she pointed out to my mother that one of my

brothers and I had left Cleveland, but *her* children could always be reached in a matter of minutes, as fast as a person could snap a dial tone, she was only naming facts. She wasn't gloating. Facts are facts, Cleveland is Cleveland. She wasn't accusing my mother of total failure. She pitied boys whose ancestors came all the way from Kamenetz-Podolsk to a wonderful place like Cleveland and still something drove them on to San Diego, San Francisco, what kind of goyish names are those?

My mother, of course, argued her side of the story and received the counsel of her big sister. Family was all. Life is clear, painful, confused, and busy. Together, the sisters fought back. Some things were better left out of the discussion, but neither of them could think of what these things might be.

"Anna, you awake?"

"In such a world, who can sleep?"

"But you stopped talking a second."

"Okay, I had a little snooze. In such a world, doesn't a person need her rest?"

My mother loved these hours with her on the telephone. A little nagging, a little nudging, a little bragging, a little complaint—a nice contact to start the morning. She always had the time, no matter how busy with her own cooking and sewing and taking care. Aunt Anna was decisive, clear, and fun, unlike other people my mother could and frequently did name. Aunt Anna sat alone in her house, good riddance to the helpers she fired, peering through the lens chunks of her glasses, talking on the telephone with the amplifier attached, occasionally eating a nice hot noodle or two if someone had dropped some by in an unmarked container, talking with her children, her sister, her nieces, her nephews, her grandchildren. The days were too short for all she had to do and all the advice which was continuously simmering. If someone tried to push her into ninety-six when she knew for a positive fact she was only ninety-five or maybe—God be praised—ninety-four, she grew vexed but it didn't last. The kids always gave in. She couldn't hold grudges. Grudges tend to age a person, and at her time in life, she didn't need to age unnecessarily.

That smile played slyly on her lips. A person smiles, she's got it figured out. Or if she hasn't, who will ever know?

Even my own children, whom she almost never saw, took a place in the system. She transmitted orders to my mother to pass on to me so that I could act on them; immediately would be best. I usually reported back with the advice to leave this stuff alone, she didn't know enough about my life, and my mother answered: "Don't get in a dignant. Far as I can see, she's more mature than lots of your cronies."

"Mother, I don't need her to tell me to make sure my former wife reminds the kids to eat a good breakfast."

"Wouldn't hurt," my mother said. "I read only yesterday one-minute oatmeal costs just five cents a serving, you can cook it in a jiffy, and the kids go away to school with a song in their heart and their galoshes on—I saw it on Channel Four."

"Mother, would you pass the word? I don't like lectures."

"Of course, I don't use the one-minute style."

"Mother—"

"I use the slow-cook old-fashion style. Personally, I want healthy kids."

"*Mother!*"

My mother translated this into language Aunt Anna could understand: They are fine, delightful, regular in habits, eat good, beautiful handwriting, and send all their love.

"Is he doing what I say?" she would ask anxiously. "I

can't be responsible, Frieda, unless he listens to me. Your Herbert was never such a good listener."

I stopped in Cleveland on my way to Haiti when I last saw her. "What you need to go to the old country?" she asked. "We got out okay, didn't we? Why you need to go back?"

"Haiti isn't the old country, Aunt Anna."

"It's over that way, isn't it? Over there? I remember the Cossacks, plus no fresh vegetables all winter, just potatoes, maybe a beet. Isn't it winter now? Are you crazy wasting your time in the old country with the Cossacks and the potatoes is all you'll get?"

"Well, I'll let you know, Aunt Anna."

"Have a good time. It's nice to travel if you're a young man. I bet nothing looks like it used to anymore. And one good thing about traveling, five is enough already these days, you can't have kids while you're traveling. Do you have a wife?"

"Not now."

"So maybe you'll find a nice one in the old country."

"That's not what I'm going for, Aunt Anna."

"Here, put your face close to me so I can see if you deserve a new wife. Let me look. Where'd you get all the hair? You need money for a haircut? Okay, I guess you better try to find one in the old country."

"A haircut?"

"A wife, dummy. But not one of those just wants a free ticket to Cleveland. They take advantage of nice young American boys in the old country. All they dream about is Cleveland. You better send me her picture first, also something about the family, a few details."

"I'm going to Haiti, Aunt Anna—"

"And get yourself a haircut or she'll think you're a bum.

130

Which would show she's got a good head on her shoulders, if your mother asks me."

She was smiling at something she was not saying and I was not answering. There was a secret life beyond her advice-giving. What passages opened in her dreaming when the house was quiet, the telephone at rest, her children not poking about, meddling and fussing, breathing up her air and bothering her thoughts? It's not just the sinus fills up in a head.

The ancient past in muddy Russia. The grit, mystery, noise, and hope of America. Where was she now? Children getting old. Babies whose names it was not necessary to remember. A husband with a head that shook—long dead. Cleveland filled with strangers and the shul where her father played checkers was not even a Baptist church anymore—a novelty shop. Another day. Another night. All this was not so bad unless you thought about it.

I knew little of my own secret thoughts below the line of rumination and desire. How should I have known hers? But there was still desire in her, an intention to improve others, an impeccable smiling rage to make things right.

She ate alone at the kitchen table. She had an idea. She picked up the phone and worked the enlarged funny-face dial. "Frieda? Frieda? Are you there, Frieda?"

The two sisters stood nearly alone against receding history. Together they remembered their mother, Hilda, the old country, the Depression, old times. When their voices sang together on the telephone, the present did not recede, their husbands were full of vigor, their sons had all their hair and promise, trouble was still to be cured by mothers who kept the remedies close by.

"Anna! It's Frieda," my mother said. "So you ate all the nice noodles Florence brought over?"

"Frieda, you want to talk serious? I heard Esther's boy is a dropout, she don't listen when I tell her, Harvard is no school for a serious student—"

"Anna, my son Herbert tells me Harvard is serious."

"Which it is the proof, Frieda. Don't he defend the Ivory League every chance he gets? When our mother said we had to come to America to get an education, she was talking Western Reserve, she was talking Ohio State, she was talking *serious*, Frieda—how's your diverticulus?"

"I'm no spring chicken, Anna."

"So what does that make me? Even a soup I'm not good for, you boil and boil, the meat gets tough—see a good stomach man, Frieda. My son the allergist and dermatology plus medical buildings says always get a second opinion."

"I got one already. They both say eat bland."

"Frieda, what do they know?"

A few weeks after I last saw her, she was moving through her house, perhaps to the sink, more likely to the telephone, and fell against the piano bench. Fell; broke her hip; thought she might die. She lay there, considering the matter, until someone found her. She was clear in her mind and annoyed. I don't know why a broken hip should be the final disaster for old people. Her son, the retired doctor, explained to me about calcium loss due to lack of exercise and nutrition and something normal in the aging process. The "immobilized geriatric"—in this case, his mother—tended to die.

Before Aunt Anna followed the normal pattern, she said goodbye, still alert and smiling and complaining about her difficulties in hearing and understanding. The smile flickered and played and she complained to her children and her surviving sister, my mother. She said she would die. She knew it was time now, no matter whether she was ninety-five or ninety-six, or even only ninety-four, as she preferred. She had a few final remarks. She waited to make sure she had forgotten nobody. And then she died.

On the telephone to San Francisco my mother said, "I was her little sister and she called me every day. She called me her little sister. I feel bad about fooling her with those fish scallop noodles but she had to eat and keep her calcium up. She was really ninety-six."

My mother is eighty-three. She says she's only eighty-two.

"I've lost my big sister," she said. "I talked to her every day. I miss her.

"Even your father," she said, "and you know he never goes out anymore, he wanted to go to her funeral. Even your father. Even your father. But your father can't know anymore how much I miss my big sister."

9 BACK IN America after her years in Israel, the daughter met a nice young doctor. The father made the head-tucked-in, double-chinned joke of a beaming and jovial parent: "She managed to find the only non-Jewish young doctor in town." The young doctor went to temple with her, and they would visit her friends in Israel on their wedding trip, and he seemed to love her.

On the day of the wedding the father, who had been happy in love but then had been unhappy, felt a gliding sensation of unreality. He saw his daughter coming to lead the life she deserved, a fine and fruitful one. He had grown unfamiliar with such prospects. The celebration in a garden contributed to this gliding vivid unreality. The daughter's mother, his first wife, was there, and also his second wife, and also his own mother, taking the busy part of grandmother of the bride, and also several women friends of his. His daughter often liked his women friends, made friends with them, teased them about her veteran father's funny habits, and asked him to marry again. *Not yet, not yet, too early, I'm still too amazed,* he said. *Why don't you get less amazed, dad?* his daughter replied.

And now his mother too, sniffing around, asking questions, her wig on straight, rustling her fancy new blue taffeta, was making declarations in a clear voice. "Nice girls, some of them. That one over there, she says you take her to the movies. Don't be shy."

"Mother," he answered, "I don't think shyness is the problem here."

"A person like you, always stayed home reading and ruining their eyes—"

"Mother, I didn't go blind."

"Then look! Take a look at that pretty one you take to the movies sometimes! Can't you see? She's over there talking to some other boy, you better pay some attention."

At his daughter's wedding there were stately skinny persons who seemed to have been washed up onto bourgeois shores when the flower children went out to sea. There were weathered young couples who had come in from their forest refuges. One of the communards from Mountain View days, 1969, was telling about Ampex, expanding his consciousness by selling recording tape, discs, and computer software to the People. *I'm in the memory business,* he explained, and the father said, *It's mutual.*

Times had changed again. The guests were wearing the goofy smiles of a celebration—true love once more. They drifted from group to group, hearty ones, giggly ones. It was Saturday afternoon and a Druidess in a filmy costume played a flute, picking up blossoms and leaves in the ends of her robe. She may not have been as tall as she imagined herself.

Dooms of love, he thought. A young woman said to him, Hello, old lover; and he answered, You mean former lover; and she smiled and kissed him and said, Hello, old former lover.

This was not a day for quibbles.

The humanist minister shook his jowls, deepened his tones, portrayed an Elizabethan adept of victuals and strong drink as he performed the ritual of passing bride to husband. He winked at the father, his old friend. Since he combined careers as minister and actor, he slid his voice down to an impressive bass for pronouncing the familiar words, using enough vibrato to pop corn, plus enough ooze to butter it. The grandmother of the bride pinched the father and whispered, "He's nice, he's good, but they could have found a nice rabbi, too."

The day was, for the father, a graduation. "Yes, here," he said to the groom, and gave away a last part of his youth.

He kissed the mother of his daughter. The light bones he hugged felt unfamiliar but friendly. The long war was ended.

He kissed the younger sister. "My turn next, dad," she said.

He kissed his own mother.

In a kissing mood, he kissed his second wife. He kissed their children. He kissed others. "Stop me before I kiss more," he said to his mother.

"Hah?" she asked. "It don't hurt to be nice. I always told you be nice. You're getting there. Now you see, you got a nice daughter and son-in-law and pretty soon, *when?* I want a grandchild for you."

"Which will be a great-grandchild for you, mother."

"Didn't I say that? Which it goes without saying. Also the in-laws are lovely people, Congolationists, did they tell you? What's that, some kind of goyim, I know, but what else?"

He continued on his kissing rounds. By mistake he kissed his oldest friend, who had introduced him to his first wife. It was getting to be a habit. His head was filled with sunlight and rum and good feeling. He wanted to explain to everyone that he now could understand why drink had come well-recommended through the centuries. It led to warm-hearted results. Usually it did. The humanist minister suggested he sit down and just preside a while. He did so.

As a tribute to him, because he had expressed strong desires in the matter, the radiant Druid flautist with leafy hems did not play "Greensleeves."

He heard insects buzzing, blood and music thrumming. He accepted congratulations. He admired the friends of his daughter and son-in-law. He observed the delicate small person in antique lace, his eldest daughter, floating among her admirers. He hoped she would remember he was the first of them.

While he suddenly felt weariness in his legs, his mother remained curious and tireless. He was also an admirer of this lady. She had many questions, many answers, and knew better than anyone how to make a question serve as an answer. Just now, nearby, she was speaking with his first wife, whom she hadn't seen in many years. "Who will eat all this food?" she asked. "Maybe," she said, smiling, intending to declare peace between parts of a family, "maybe you could take some in a few jars and containers, would you like that, dear?"

"We don't carry food with us on trips," the first wife said, holding the arm of her husband, softening the reproach in honor of the occasion: "Mother."

"What kind of snacks they got in a motor hotel you're staying in I suppose, if you get hungry in the night?"

"We don't get hungry in the night. We're staying at the Fairmont."

"Is that nice? They got parking, too? They got a breakfast place, a brunch place?"

"You don't have to worry, mother."

"You're right I suppose," said the former mother-in-law. She turned to the former wife's husband, including him in a nostalgic moment of reconciliation. "She's right I'm sure, isn't she? In America we don't need to go hungry very much, unless we're always on a diet."

There were lanterns swinging from the branches of fruit trees, there was music, there was a long day washing into a California sunset. The photographer in a long gown took pictures of the new couple, and also of the father of the bride with his first wife, his second wife, his mother, his daughters, and his women friends. Occasional errors of calibration occurred when guests stood toe-to-toe for civilities with these women. One of the father's friends, pointing to the first wife, asked, "Why'd she walk away in the middle of my telling her what a fine fellow you are?"

"Beats me," he said.

"She turned red, besides. It wasn't a time to blush."

"You're a good and tactful observer," he said. "On this sentimental occasion I deeply appreciate your friendship over the years. Just don't speak well of me to that lady."

"She's the mother of the bride."

"And I'm the father. It's a coincidence. One of those accidents that happens. We're making the best of it."

"Ah. Oh. Good food. Love that fruit salad."

"Have you met my mother?"

"Oh, man—lively. Now there's someone doesn't walk away in the middle of a discussion. I met her at the cheese, where she told me your life story. Say, you must be a pretty interesting fellow to raise a mother like that—"

The party was dangerous fun, like a fruit salad soaked with bottles of kirsch. A friend and he put arms around each other's shoulders a moment, a hero's marching-to-battle gesture, into the sunset, grown children, the battle not yet over, and then separated as if by centrifugal force or the call of a spouse. Both had children; neither had a spouse. They crunched fallen apples underfoot.

Oh there it goes. "Greensleeves." The lovely flautist was her own person, and had her own repertory. Or maybe the People had made a request. The former communard, now in software at Ampex, was trailing after her, offering memory bank and recall discs and miniaturization as he once offered psylocibin and Owsley Blues.

The kirsch, the rum, the heat of the afternoon. The family, the friends, the garden smells trampled by crowd. Crushing made the flowers give up their sweetness all at once; the apples, too. The day. The happiness. Within the heat radiating out from his cheeks and temples, there was also the visible and invisible aura of the past. A crushing seemed to bring forth, all at once, the sadness. There were ghosts, the ghosts of the living, of what they once were, darker and more haunting than the ghosts of the dead; the ghost of love sometimes felt, not felt any longer, and still aching (as amputated limbs are said to ache); the ghost of his father, wandering in a hallway, alive and sick of being nine-

139

ty years old in Cleveland; the ghostly histories of loved women and friends and children in this garden, the aura of the past. There was also the ghost of the future and the still possible, the conceivable, the intentional, the accidental, the blessings and bounty of dream. He even thought he saw Hilda, his mother's mother, in her Russian dress, the skirts spreading; her smile hilarious and secretly entertained, like his Aunt Anna's smile, like his mother's sometimes, like the smile on the face of his grandmother in old photographs— no, her mouth was severe in those photographs; only *now* was she smiling.

Of course, no one else saw Hilda, gone for more than half a century, and his vision of mother, grandmother, great-grandmother, was nothing to be proud of, unless a father should be proud of drinking well at a feast in honor of his firstborn daughter.

The father wished his daughter's wedding day could go on and on, and this garden might spin slowly as it was now spinning, with flute music playing and good wishes heavily banked against whatever bad wishes might be floating in the summer air. He almost believed there were none. Youth was lovely and age was good and the complicated company here present was at peace. Those who stayed late gazed with the purposeless liquid beauty of eyes at a wedding, that brimming of feeling which is empty of content and filled with all meanings. No wonder everyone looked fascinating and healthy! They were believing in love and denying history. Like them, even more than the others, the father beamed and beamed, and wanted to be nothing more than a father; today, being a father summed up everything for him, he was a father.

He was a son. His mother's breasts, normally hidden, made themselves flirtatiously evident behind noisy blue taffeta. She loved a wedding. Her activity on its behalf transmitted an interest in love which never gave up. She admitted persistent rumors of old age, but you know how people gossip. Her eyes laughed and appealed to everyone, and nearly everyone here responded to her need—loved her.

It was her business to live at a high pitch. Public festivals suited her. Family doesn't always accept this overflow; family can become a ward; it's everything, and yet it confines. "My mother always liked parties, too. Her name was Hilda —seems like a German name, I don't know why. She was a sociable person. Of course, in her day, we kept to our own, we didn't have such big doings, we couldn't afford so much extra waste, for instance—the fruit salad alone!" The voice confided secrets and truths. It went from listener to listener, careless and flirtatious and happy. It told her life story, her mother Hilda, her sister Anna, her husband, our city of Cleveland, her children, her grandchildren to come, her sick husband, who had become older than either of them wanted him to be; she offered advice, based, as she said, on a little bit of experience which could not be denied; she judged freely and robustly, needing little evidence, and before she left a conversation, she asked her interlocutor to repeat his or her name. "Spell it, please. That's a nice name —Catholic? Some very good people, I'm sure. Like some very nice colored I met through my son the writer. Spell it. At my age, which is seventy plus I won't tell you how many, maybe more, the memory gets overcrowded."

She wanted to stay till dark, when the lanterns would be lit.

Like her son, she wanted the day never to end. Her son said to her, "I wish dad could have come out for this."

"He can't. He can't anymore."

"We should have just insisted. You see old people on planes all the time."

Her lips were pressed together and white. "What're you going to do with all this food? People can't eat all this. I suppose the caterer gets to take it home."

"I wonder what dad's thinking."

"It'll spoil in the sun. It'll spoil unless you get it into a cooler. He's not thinking at all, maybe just when to take his pills."

"No, he knows everything."

"He tell you he's afraid of the dark now? Also did he tell you that?"

"Mother, he knows everything."

Of course he's afraid of the dark. That's because he knows.

"There's all this intermarriage between men and women these days," his mother said. "Look at them here. Everyplace you look there's this intermarriage. But her husband is a nice steady fellow anyway, won't they be happy, I'll have a great-grandchild soon, won't I? When, do you think? What will they do with all this extra California fruit salad? Even a king doesn't waste so much."

For a time at a wedding, standing in groups with food and drink and smiles and garden smells, the celebrants were relieved of their ocean solitudes; they were no longer shipwrecked in the world; it seemed that God intended them to nourish themselves and others, talking and laughing and looking into the light of another happy eye. There was summer in their hair and summer in their faces, summer smells when they breathed closely and laughingly upon each other. Today the father believed God had intentions and good ones. The father felt he too had fulfilled these good intentions today, and regret seized him only as his glance fell on his former wives—then he realized he had loved them and it was okay, for the moment it was okay—and then the sadness insisted its way back on a traveled path because his own father was alive and alone thousands of miles away, unable to take his part in the spiral of generations. The part he now took could not be justified by thoughts of evening, of gentleness, of inexorability. Not okay, and the sadness did not give place to anything, it was merely pain and the end of hopes for an old man.

Nevertheless, the father of the bride was happy for his daughter. He was happy enough; regret performed no useful labor; he decided to be happy.

"She got some nice friends," his mother reported. She had made forays of investigation and discussion. "Some of them your friends, some of them her friends, it's all mixed up in California. In our city of Cleveland you can tell whose friend is whose."

"It doesn't make any difference," he said.

His mother rustled her taffeta. She straightened her Sunburst Glory hair. Circling a garden, discussing and discussing, was hard work. "Of course, in our city of Cleveland we do a lot with family. We stick to our own more. But she got a lot of friends, all kinds, I think it's very interesting. That colored in the white suit—says his father's a doctor, okay, but his mother, also! Not in our city. But he's a nice refined boy. In our city of Cleveland we wouldn't do it like this."

The sun went down. The garden began to empty. The women he had sometimes lived with or traveled with shunned the man they had in common, but smiled shyly at each other, like sisters; not like sisters, since real sisters don't do so much shy inquiring smiling at each other. One was short, slight, and angry despite her sociable smiles and

143

cigarettes; another was rangy, bony, and handsome, and moderately indifferent to him; others were fond. About each other, they were curious. They turned at the celebration like fish slowly making the warm rounds of a pond. Occasionally they were sped on their way by his mother, asking questions and making statements.

The father, former husband, former husband again, faced by all these women, made jokes and uttered comments. They gave him to understand he was not a boy anymore, although he was still a son.

The old mother, mother to the father, kept saying, "Bee-yootiful, but who can eat so much all this food on a warm day like this?"

She didn't expect an answer. Neither did the father expect more than a comment or a joke in answer to his sincere comments and jokes. He kissed his daughter. He kissed all his children. He kissed his son-in-law. He kissed his mother. He kissed his first wife. He kissed his second wife. She said to him, "I hope nobody around here brought herpes to the party."

"Good friend," he said, "I'm sorry you learned smartass from me."

Finally the sun was gone, the paper lanterns were lit, and his mother sighed blissfully, "Aah! Even in our city of Cleveland there's nothing so beautiful. Was this professional union catering?"

The day ended. The bride and groom disappeared. (Some goodbyes need no ceremony.) He explained to his mother how it was the custom to slip away. His second daughter took his mother off for further discussions.

He borrowed his youngest daughter for company—a bridesmaid she was, and still holding mashed posies in her fist. He told about her big sister's folding the napkins on her kibbutz during the October war, because people deserved a nice table, and the child replied gravely, "I do that, too." They drove back to the city together and he delivered her to her mother, the one who liked jokes.

And then he went to bed alone. He brushed his teeth, put his suit on hangers (his second wife, who liked to tease, suggested he give this suit to Goodwill), put away his tie, telephoned to make sure his mother was comfortable, and wondered if he was doing things in the proper order. For a bachelor any order seems to do. He proposed to himself the interesting question: should he be going to bed alone? Today? Tonight? Surely not, he thought; many nights are bitterly uneasy for a man curled up around no one. But then he came to an interesting result when he examined how he felt about the question: today and tonight he didn't mind. He felt no grief. There was still love in the universe, that wedding garden had been drenched with it, and he could wait his turn again.

He telephoned to make sure his mother was comfortable. She said, "I just talked to you already. Are you going to have a hangover tomorrow? Take two aspirin right now and drink some Vee-eight."

He remembered a dog on a picnic and his mother's determination.

He sank into sleep with the grateful sigh of a man for whom, despite everything, even despite himself, things turn out well in the end. *In the end*, of course is only an expression. Each end is the beginning of something else.

10   I was taking my father down from Shaker Heights to the office where he would meet his partner, who had already met with accountants and lawyers, to settle the details. He was officially signing his retirement from business. He was admitting the facts. This morning the traffic was heavy with Cleveland commuting, a solemn, gray, slow procession at rush hours, and I was impatient behind the wheel. Why was I driving? He used to drive, and he used to be patient behind the wheel. In my boyhood, the skies were mostly clear—or so I remembered them—clean snow and clean rains, clean clouds, heavy Lake Erie sunlight, and sometimes on the way downtown we stopped to swim at Edgewater or Gordon Park in the black lake. Now not.

"This way," he said. "Then turn left."

"When?"

"I'll tell you," he said.

"What street's it on?" I asked.

He sat in silence. After a while he said, "Isn't that funny, I been going there more than fifty years and I forget the street. It'll come to me." He waited. "I been going there more than fifty years and it didn't come to me yet."

"That's all right, dad, I forget everything, too. It's what you have a secretary for."

He didn't reply. He didn't believe me, either.

"That way," he said. We recognized the street at the same time. "Rockwell and Twelfth," he said. "Park in there."

I helped him out. Legs first, then hand on hips, pushing, then straightening up. He observed carefully. He made no comment on the procedure. Over his face was fitted the mask of Parkinson's disease, of a stroke, the fixedness of an Oriental totem somehow removed to the erosions of Cleveland, Ohio. *Rockwell and Twelfth.* His lips moved silently, making sure for next time.

We were at an intersection of warehouses, offices, residence hotels by the week or the month, candidates for "urban renewal." My father knew his way here. He knew who owned what, and where the city would condemn, where the developers might build, and how to thread among the bricks and dust, the writeoffs, the leasebacks. His partner, my mother's brother Dave, had always deferred to my father in this enterprise. Personally, he preferred his other business—electrical. He found electrical classier than real estate—cleaner, and a person dealt with classy business school graduates from New York, Michigan, and Illinois.

147

Electrical had always been good to him. A shrewd, pink-faced person with a dapper mustache, a smell of aftershave, a few million dollars, he was only five or six years younger than my father. He lacked a few diseases. He still quarrelled with his eldest son, unlike my father. He wanted to run everybody's life. He used to defer to Sam in real estate, but no more. "Sell it, whatever we can get," he said.

"This is not a good time. The price is terrible. If I was well, I'd fix it up, it's a good property," my father said.

"You're not well, Sam."

"Things can't get worse, can they?"

Silence. The pink-faced partner and brother-in-law stuck the desk pen into its holder with a little popping noise, removed it with a little sucking one. A bronzeoid plaque on the desk pen said: FEDERAL INSULATION SINCE 1921. My father's partner said, "What else can we do, Sam? You got no options."

The silent lawyer in the room sighed. He saw his commissions floating and bobbing on the inertia of my father's weaknesses. My father looked at the sigh; he probably saw a shadow on another chair; he turned his fist in his hand. "Sell it," he said. "I won't get well for a long time. We might as good close down. Rockwell and Twelfth."

"What you say, Sam?"

"Just thinking, Dave. Sell it."

I went out to talk with my cousins, Dave's sons, middle-aged boys like me. There were tables of decorator formica in blond wood colors. International Gallery paintings hung on my uncle's office walls—good enough for business. At home, he let his wife buy Art; here, the decorator took care of it. One of my cousins said my father still had all his marbles and I said, You bet, and my cousin said, Just a little fading is all.

148

I went back in. He needed family nearby. The lawyer was spreading papers on the table for him to sign. The partner's mustache was lifted at the corners in a small mustache smile. My father was perched on his chair like a gray doll, waiting for the pen to be presented to him. His elbows were close to his side and his chin was down. He had a habit of rapid fading like this. My cousin was right. The blood left his face. But he still had his marbles, or at least knew where they were. Or at least knew where and when and how they were missing, and that he regretted this.

The haunted death look in the eyes, seeming to follow the course of the drugs through his body, chemical sweepers, stimulaters, dissolvers, calmers, was succeeded by an icily dim look, fragile, transparent, and as terrifying as the Arctic. I couldn't choose between them. They explored different griefs, and marooned him in different ways.

"What if he just stopped taking the drugs?" I asked.

Shoulders lifted. That was impossible. (Why?) The doctors with their prescriptions stitched a sort of life together in the irregular heart, the uninsulated nerves, the twitching riddle of Parkinsonism, the giddiness without fun, the glacier-crowded brain, the frozen arteries.

"He's not himself," I said.

"Who is he then?" my mother asked. "I have to call that my husband now. That's your father."

"So shouldn't he just not take the medicines?"

My mother leaned back and sighed. "Years ago, everybody said you should be a doctor. Now, at your age, all at once you're a physician and surgeon?"

I would wait and follow orders, like everyone, and dislike the orders, like everyone. I took vitamins, didn't I? my mother reminded me, and who knows what's right?

My father's description of his first stroke was bemused and proud, and he meant to make us laugh. "I leaned forward on my desk. I was negotiating. Morris Geller, a bad negotiator. I went black, but I didn't let him know—he takes advantage. He thought I was thinking. Then I came back and I made a good deal. Later the doctors got a picture inside what happened to me, but Morris Geller never knew."

He used to look for a reflection of the joke in my face when he told this story. But now when we talked, he didn't look into my eyes. He couldn't see well enough, of course, but also he preferred not to open the window and let me see too much; tomorrow maybe, not today—save something for tomorrow or my next visit to Cleveland.

For a seder, which he treated as another meal, he raised himself up through the scaffolding. He told the old stories. He grinned. The gray eyes thawed as if he could see to the end of the table. He was not controlled by conditions. "I should of gone to the wedding. Now I decide." He decided to be a father again, and asked, "So what's going on? Tell me. Tell me loud, I want to hear."

Later, when everyone had gone to bed, the house creaking into silence, he hung back, wanting to talk. He had a confession for me. He was shy about it. "Don't have too good a memory," he said. "I remember the bottom, not the top. Like one of them skyscrapers downtown on Euclid, nighttime. The lobby is lit. The offices are dark."

"What are you remembering, dad?"

"I got gaps. I got blooey places, like my eyes."

"But you're thinking about something now."

"I used to make her laugh, your mother. I chased a guy away with my fruit hammer. We used to yell a lot, but she didn't . . ." He was shaking his head.

150

"She's hard on you. I know, dad. It's hard for her, too."

"What you call it? Scalds me."

"I know, dad." He meant scolds, scolds.

"I can't talk back. I don't even remember the lobby so good. I don't know why she laughed at my tricks. I'm tired. What else can I be?"

He waited for me to answer. He used to wait for me to take over the business; he used to shout at me for my stupidity when I said no. Now he waited to see if I had an answer to the question. *What else, what next?* I had no answer. When I came to see him, flying from California or from New York, he asked, "Are you staying?"

"I'm staying a few days, dad."

"Try to stay a little longer next time, Herbert."

And I felt a stab (who cares what I felt?) and said, "Well, my children are back in San Francisco, dad, and I've got work to do." He could understand that. He tried to understand that.

And on the day I left he got up early, speaking in that thin deaf old man's voice, "Thanks for coming." He did not reproach me for leaving so soon. I said I'd be back in a few months. He said nothing. This man who never used to demonstrate love with his body now liked to be tucked in, helped to move, kissed. I kissed him goodbye and will not describe his breath or the feel of his skin.

The next time I came to see him, the doctors thought he had suffered another "ministroke." What's that? I asked a doctor who was asking my father what color his eyes are, who is the President.

"The arteries are tired. Sometimes they leak. I hate to say break. Dad's getting on."

"What kind of doctor are you?"

151

"I practice psychiatry. I did my neurological boards, so I have a double specialty. Dad's going to need help, Herbert. Old age is a coming problem in our country."

On a temporary basis, until he got back on his feet, the family hired a nurse. She drove up in an enormous black convertible Buick Skylark, freshly washed so that the rust spots, dents, and ragged edges shined, and the torn canvas was still wet. Flossie herself, gleamy, glossy, and sharp in a white uniform, said, "I'm your Home Visiting,"—smiles, healthy arms, glitter of good health in the eyes, plus brains and good nature. "Visiting Nurse for Hire is what I do."

"Well-recommended, I'm sure," said my mother. "I'm the wife—head of the home now. This is the sick man."

My father was propped in his chair, politely waiting. Flossie turned to him. "You can speak okay?"

My mother whispered. "He has trouble with his functions. You got to keep him clean. I been doing it personally. He used to be a very clean individual."

"Course I can speak! I know everything!" he burst out. "Don't talk about me like that!"

"He don't like us to talk about him," my mother confided. "He's sensitive like a baby—didn't used to be like that."

"Mr. Gold!" Flossie said. "You play cards?"

"He can't see the cards. He can't hear you," my mother said.

"You play rummy?" my father asked. "I think I can play rummy pretty good. I hear everything Flossie says."

"Good, good, I like rummy," Flossie said. "Let's deal right here on your lap."

"Use the tray," my mother said.

My brothers and I left Flossie and dad to get acquainted. Mother watched from the doorway. I tried to pull her away. She shook off my arm. "Mother!" I said.

"How come he hears this Flossie talk," she asked, "and he don't hear me?"

"Mother, I'm hungry," I said, and only with this emergency—a son in need of food—would she leave them alone while she dealt out a snack in the kitchen. She discussed keeping alive until dinner, bread tomatoes and cheese versus cold meat cucumbers rolls, or maybe a little pickled fish from the jar? And she discussed the numerous flaws of this here Flossie, who would spoil him, make him into a baby—a grown man he was supposed to be. She lectured and fed and was unhappy.

My father said he couldn't see the cards well enough. Flossie insisted he could see and she would tell him his cards so he could pick if he couldn't see. "But then you know my hand."

"I forget, Mr. Gold. My God, this here a *game!* Time you learn it all a *game*, Mr. Gold."

He smiled. "Come on and play, Flossie."

"Then we shave you. Then we take care of other things."

"What's this red picture card, hearts or diamonds?"

"Jack of Heart."

"I knew that, Flossie. Just wanted to hear if you tell the truth." He held the card to his chest. "What is it?"

"Forgot. Didn't I tell you?"

His mouth came open. There was no sound, but I could see an old shape of my father's uproariousness, laughing over the cards with his cronies, the joke on everybody.

It turned out there was money in the family. He had always played his cards close to the chest, but now we had to see and we didn't forget. Oddly enough, faced by all the problems, taxes and such, fair division of more money than we expected, the brothers and the mother came to an agreeable idea. He could give much of it to good causes, a hospital, Jewish welfare, Israel, ideas and causes which gave him satisfaction. My father said that was okay and when the time came. . . . The time was now, we insisted. We didn't like to talk about estate taxes, but we did. It was important right now.

"I give," he said.

"Let's give more," I said. "It makes sense to do it while people can still say thank you."

"I don't have to hear thank you. I always give enough."

"Dad," I said, "we all feel you shouldn't try to leave it to us. Give more now—*you* give it."

He didn't understand. He didn't like what he heard. Perhaps he wanted to continue holding what was his, or to control it through his sons, his grandchildren. He had spent a long life working; the rewards had given his life measurable value. Sometimes we spoke these matters while Flossie, who worked for twenty-eight dollars a day, pulled his toes or fingers, washed him, cleaned his ears with Q-tips, helped him. "We all agree, dad," I repeated.

And he answered stubbornly, "How much can a man give? Right, Flossie?"

"I wasn't listening, Mr. Gold," she said.

"You heard," he said. "How much can a man give?"

"Up to you," she said.

"See?" he asked us as we closed around his chair. "She got respect for a man. She don't talk to accounts and lawyers. They don't know what I got in mind."

Dad, we said, the taxes. Dad, we said, these are charities you like. Dad, we said, we want you to do what you really want to do.

"Then listen to me," he said. "I give already. Stop hammering."

154

Mother hammered. Once her mind fastened on giving away money to important causes, and incidentally not permitting the government to steal it, she wanted the matter taken care of and she wanted it taken care of today. But it required a signature by the competent owner and giver. Her husband was the owner. He refused to sign. "I'm charitable," he said. "I believe in charity. But how much can a man give? And don't I have children and grandchildren I been saving up for?"

Dad, we said, we don't need it. It's better this way, dad. Let's explain it again—

"He's not listening," my mother said. "Sam! You're not listening!"

"I heard already. Flossie, put a pillow right here. My back is kind of blooey today. Oh, that's better. Thank you, Flossie."

Rage and generosity played turbulently in my mother's heart. An epidemic of giving away money had swept the family, rushing around my father. Get rid of this stuff, lest it cause trouble among us. Get it out, so the accountants and lawyers would not rule. It was a peculiar climax in the commercial life of a family, and to my father, for whom money had been a token of security—he was never greedy —it seemed incomprehensibly like ingratitude. Why give away what he had sacrificed so much for? In his weakness we wanted to throw his money back in his face. Wouldn't that leave the family defenseless, as he had been, a green boy in America, not speaking the language, without family, knowing nothing but the imperative to survive? Were we telling him he had made a wrong turn forever ago, and nothing to be done about it now but to junk the gain?

"Dad, these are good things. Dad, these are things you

155

give to anyway. Dad, there's enough for us. Dad, the government will grab it otherwise."

He seemed to listen. He fell silent and brooding. Stiff and white and the blood gone from his face, he stared into space. He seemed to be listening and he was not listening. He asked again, "How much can a man give?" and then turned to me. Having completed the question, he awaited my answer.

"You've given a lot, dad. We all know that."

He shook his head. It was useless to explain about trusts and estate laws. He had kept it snug for us, and now ingratitude, even from his eldest son, father of his grandchildren; that was what he knew. Behind glaucoma, deafness, angina, Parkinsonism, spinal arthritis, swollen prostate, arteriosclerosis, and a sane and sensible grief concerning these ills, he made out dim echoes down the congested hallways: ungrateful, ingrates, impatient children, angry wife, everything slipping away, everyone gone.

He had taught me to ice skate at City Ice & Fuel, and he paid for hot chocolate after he paid both adult's and children's admissions, and I loved skating because he and my mother had first met, they said, at the ice skating rink at East 105th and Euclid.

He rode my first children on the handlebars of his bicycle when he was seventy-five and I was already saying, "As I enter middle age . . ."

"What's that?" he asked. "Why not me? You copy other people?" Now we were copying other sons, his future widow was full of resentment, he was copying other old men in not understanding what had been done to them.

He had cataracts on both eyes, and he was ninety, and anyway, they weren't ripe yet—*ripe* is the word the ophthamologist used—so they couldn't be peeled off even if he

156

could bear the operation. I believed he would see the world better if he could see the world. He could still understand. He was locked in that dull frozen melancholia partly from the drugs he took and partly from the failure of his senses. He couldn't hear. He couldn't see. His mind was troubled, but not absent. He was locked away by his body; his soul knew it was locked away.

"I see blur," he said. "It's blur."

He had a special lamp to read by. It was a strong circle of fluorescent light, very ugly strong light, around his large magnifying glass. With it, perhaps he could read, but he didn't know how to turn the frame on its swivel so that he could use the glass. He tried to read the headlines with the light, a kind of halo above his dreaming face, but he didn't use the glass. I swiveled it around to show him how it worked. "Now put it back," he said. I put it back. "You see, it's easy," I said. "How does it work?" he asked. I did it again. "Now put it back," he said.

"Now you do it, dad."

He tried to force it backwards. No, no, the other way. He got it right this time. "Now put it back," he said.

"You see, you can read."

A moment later he was peering at the headlines without the benefit of the glass. He didn't trust it. He didn't like it. He denied it.

I asked him to use the glass.

"It's all right," he said. "I'm tired. I'm a little tired. I'm going to take a little nap. Everything I see is blur."

The face of childhood, eyes frowning, lips pouting, the gaze withdrawn and dry, without tears, lips pushed out—I had seen this in men facing death in war. I saw it in my father as he became a child in the face of a quarrel he could not win. "Isn't Flossie coming tomorrow? Tomorrow

Wednesday? I need her every day, not just three times week, she covers me when I sleep, but your mother wanted to fire her. But *she* won't cover me. So I said Flossie got to be here two-three times week at least, things to do for me, it's hard otherwise—"

My brother Sid came to cover him at night. When I was visiting I covered him. He sighed and curled up, not needing to say thank you. When he had a bad dream and we heard him groaning, we returned to his room to cover him again.

So far he was still cashing in some gains, and no one could take Flossie from him—not on Monday, Wednesday, and Friday, anyway. And he hadn't signed any papers yet. He knew we could do nothing, it was all still his, until he signed.

Sid picked me up at Cleveland Hopkins Airport, which was also the site of a federal experimental aviation laboratory, and of the gourmet Airport Holiday Inn, named by *Cleveland Magazine* as one of the finest spots for dining in the Cleveland area. We drove through Brookpark, across railway tracks, roundabout through Parma, on the circuitous routes he chose so we could talk a while and I could come down to the reality of my native place. A set of smokestacks sent inky black and furry yellow into the sky. "The Ford Smokeless Foundry," my brother said.

"Wouldn't allow that where I live," I said.

"It was advertised as Advanced State of the Art Smokeless," he said. "They've taken down the billboard."

We both coughed. He enjoyed his continuing close examination of our hometown. He was close to the Hillbilly Maoists who marched through Polish and Hungarian neighborhoods, shouting, "Down with the Trotskyite

Revisionists!" People concerned only with their gardens, their Social Security payments, their children, and keeping the blacks at bay could not be roused by the writings of Chairperson Mao. "End Pig Brutality," the slogan engraved by a Cornell literature major on his banner, earned no points for urban guerrillas on Murray Hill, an embattled Italian enclave. West Virginia miners, come to toil in the Ford Smokeless Foundry or Republic Steel or Sherwin-Williams Paints, lantern-jawed, blue-eyed, called Floyd and Earl and Billy Don, expressed little concern with the Cultural Revolution or the treason of the Socialist Workers Faction. . . . Our father's Cleveland of old-world entrepreneurs, hammers in their pockets, loud lunches on Short Vincent Street, pride in befriending gangsters but not being one, was rapidly disappearing. Now Cleveland was either poor and troubled or rich, managerial, and corporate.

"How is he?" I asked.

"He's not going to get any better."

"Mother's still angry?"

"Doesn't want to get used to it. Stubborn used to work for her, but this time it isn't working."

"What about Flossie?"

"One of these days, gonna be gone. Mother wants dad for herself, but she wants him like he was, like he's never going to be that way again. But she still thinks dad might rise up on her if she tries to fire Flossie—"

"What's over there?"

My brother said, "That used to be a neighborhood. It's Hiroshima now. Been nuked out, you know? Redevelopment passed through here."

And then up the hill, the geological beginnings of the Allegheny mountains, a glacial bulge turning under the city, to Shaker Heights.

Before I took dad to the doctor, Flossie gave me a folded sheet of paper. "Now you make sure you show doctor this letter I wrote," she said. "You may read it, too." She leaned over my father and said firmly into his ear, knowing just how loud so that he would understand her, "Now you do what doctor says. I tole him you behave yourself, Mr. Gold, but you got to listen to doctor."

He nodded and smiled at her. She brushed back his hair with her hand and he smiled again. "That Flossie," he said. "She's crazy."

"She's nice, dad."

"She's crazy."

"Now I'm just doin' my job, Mr. Gold. You got to listen to me when doctor ain't here."

"I listen, don't I?"

She said to me, "He's good. He real good most of the time."

My mother was standing in the doorway. "That's what you say. You don't have to live with him day in and out. You don't know him."

"I work for him," Flossie said. "I got an idea."

"You work for us," my mother said, "but you don't have to live with him like I do. You should of known him when he was really a man."

"Stop fighting," my father said. "Herbert, you stop them fighting."

"No," said Flossie, "I didn't work for you then. Wasn't my job. But I reckon he's a good man—you had a good man, Mrs. Gold."

He took mood-lifters for the day, chloral hydrate at night, the bottle to be hid from him "in case of accident," the ration of jelly capsules slippery and green and doled into an Israel bonds ashtray. He gulped and suckled as he tried to swallow them. He always hated medicine and refused it. Now he asked impatiently for his pills—"what time is it? is it time yet?"—and labored like a hungry infant to take them down.

Dr. Melvin Susser, the psychiatrist, very short—"you're small but perfectly formed," I wanted to assure him—smoked nervously, extended the butt, put it back in his mouth, snorted from it, extended it again. He smiled reassuringly. "Very good results from the medication," he said. "Dad has largely unimpaired intelligence except for the depression, the pain, the sensory deprivation due to his percent deafness and near blindness. Input is lacking for dad. I think dad will be up and at 'em when we've finished with him, maybe a few office shocks I want to give him, a little course to irrigate the mentality. Then dad won't even want to see me. Dad'll be too busy, too many things to do."

"Is that a good idea?"

"I have some literature for you, Herbert. In cases of senile depression, I mean old age, you read this paper, please. It's not snakepit stuff. It's like you kick the radio and it works. It sort of irrigates. You jar the wires. What we know is the following about dad: it works."

"I don't like it."

"You got a better idea? You gonna hang around and live with his depression, Herbert?"

Dr. Susser had found rare Walter Keane paintings of large-eyed children to give his office some style. The curtains were drawn; the air conditioner hummed; there was a parking lot outside the medical building, shared with a shopping center. He stabbed out his cigarette into a ceramic ashtray depicting a molded husk of ceramic brain with geographic areas in shiny pink and gray.

"Is he going to feel better?"

161

"Dad is a leetle bit allergic to our mood enhancers, so I've taken him off them. The kidneys, just a leetle. To be on the safe side. But the shock will irrigate dad's mentality and you won't know him, dad will be so good."

He raised his voice. "Mr. Gold! What color are your eyes?"

"I suppose blue."

"Why do you say suppose?"

"It's one thing I don't worry about. People used to tell me blue."

"Okay."

"Or gray."

"Okay. I guess that's it."

He pushed against the chair and stood up without help. I asked him, "Dad, why don't you try taking longer steps?"

"Hold my arms, both of you," he said to my brother and me. Then he turned slowly to the psychiatrist. "I used to like getting up in the morning better than anything else. Now it feels so good when I just sink down. I feel myself falling asleep. Why is it I like that better than anything?"

"That's a question I can't answer," said the doctor. "You know what you feel."

"Maybe you're tired," I said.

"Tired," he said. "Something new. I'll take that treatment, doctor."

I handed Dr. Susser the letter from Flossie, my father's last love. She had told me I could read it, too.

> Patient depress. Like short walks. Like to sit with his children. Can dress self, but like to be dress. . . . Don't hear or see good, but know what goin on if he hear or see it. *Patient need help.*

"He smiled for you, didn't he?" mother asked me. "Didn't he smile?"

"Yes."

She sat with her legs apart, stumpy supports under her, the orange of her elastic garment showing, the armor she needed to keep her veins in place; fiercely, proudly, angrily, she said, "For me he hasn't put a smile on his face in three-four years—more! I said to him many times, Sam, smile a little! Why don't you smile?"

He couldn't hear when several people were speaking, and when there were all the daytime noises, traffic on the street up the hill outside, refrigerator, a TV in another room, but he knew we were talking about him. "My eyes hurt," he said.

"Smile, Sam!"

"Let's go for a walk."

We got up and made the preparations—hat, coat, keys, promises. We would be back in twenty minutes, of course. "Say goodbye to me, Sam!" my mother called.

Without looking back, he seemed to hear her. "I already did," he said.

He wore a brace for his back. His shoes were worn from shuffling, strangely natty little thin-soled black shoes, making tiny steps. I looked at his shoes and remembered the June bugs, their silky wings, that swarmed from the lake—we called them Canadian soldiers—and covered the ground for a day or two; he used to race, and ran laughing as I puffed behind him, until one summer I was able to run faster than he could. Now he tried to push through a door which wasn't quite there yet. A few steps further on I opened the door and he paused. "Walk through it," I said. I didn't want him to hang on my arm. I thought it was better for him to walk by himself.

"Mother," he said, and I knew the recital was beginning. "She's so bad now. I can't defend. Maybe she was always bad, but I didn't notice, I could defend."

"She's tired," I said. "You know she's eighty-two."

"She tells you eighty-two? I happen to know she's eighty-three."

"She's got a right to be tired, too, dad."

"I'm older. I worked all my life. So she's tired?" he asked. "I'm sick. I don't know if I'll get better, son. I had to have a rubber sheet, so she looked for bargains. She got a twin-size and what I need is a bigger size and she blames me if her bargain don't work. Why didn't she get the best one they got? Don't I deserve the best?"

"You sure do, dad."

"If I get better I'll go for a trip, a cruise. By myself. But right now I can't do without her, that's the trouble." He turned the milky gray eyes on me and I thought I saw the old light in them. "My nurse I found when I got sick, I'll take her. Can you take a black girl on a cruise?"

"Why don't you get her to be your nurse a few hours every day, dad?"

"You think mother would allow that? She's so jealous, plus tight." But there was a glint of pride in his eyes, behind the damage of glaucoma and cataract. "What she used to be was jealous and I think she still is." He looked at me shrewdly. Perhaps he only saw a shadow, but he knew who was there. "So far it don't look like you did better with women than I did. One wife in Chicago, one in California, and now you got no wife at all. As long as I wasn't sick, she was a good wife."

"She's older now, dad."

"I think she's getting old. I think that's the trouble," he

said. "I think, if I get better, I'll say I got to go on a cruise by myself. You had enough walking?"

"Are you tired, dad?"

"Not me. Let's go all the way."

I don't know if it was a phase in the spansules he was taking. He lifted his feet. I think it was not the drugs but his soul. He was really walking, not shuffling. He felt good.

"Nice to get outside," he said. "This weather. I get tired of the house. Stuffy in there. If I could breathe a sea wind, a cruise, I'd get better. That nurse Flossie and one of those things, they fold over, they fall, you got to lay just right—a deck chair—I'd get well."

"You feel better now, dad."

"Why not? I'm glad you're here. I got to talk sometimes about things, don't I? She asked me to say goodbye to her and I said I already did but I didn't, you notice, son? It's hard for me to fight back, but I can still do it."

His fists were clenched. I touched his hands to release the trigger. Gradually as I held his hand the fists relaxed and the small gray paw hung slightly turned as we walked. The shape of the eyes was the old shape of an alert animal's eyes, but within the socket, the light was shaded. When I spoke, he didn't seem to hear. He had his own thoughts. When I insisted, speaking sharply, "Are you hungry, dad?" he answered, "Yes, I remember."

Sometimes it was deafness and sometimes it was a stubborn sinking into thoughts he could not utter. He was staring straight ahead at what interested him. His eyes needed no focus. His face was shaded like a map with inaccurate use of his Remington razor, bristles defiant, nose and neck hairs long, ear hairs, a ravaged chart of a head. "You want to tell me you got a girlfriend you date?" he asked.

"I've got no announcements to make," I said.

He made that open-mouthed silent laugh with the silver minnows darting. "I bet you're like me in this regard. You don't like aggravation, but you find some."

"I'll bet."

"Let's go all the way around the block. Mother don't have to serve dinner on the dot. I like a nice day like this."

We walked.

"You remember Weinberg?" he asked suddenly. We were in front of a house with a FOR LEASE sign on it, the door open, a real estate lady showing people in. "Come on. Weinberg lived here." We walked through the flat while the real estate lady stood aside, wondering what we were looking for.

"Someone my father knew," I said.

"He left everything to that young man," my father said, "that fifty-year-old young man he always called his nephew." He looked at me and winked, and the eyes glistened. "Best nephew he ever had," he said. "Now I better go home."

He was pleased to be able to show me the neighborhood. To take the lead. To make a joke.

I telephoned one of my brothers, Eugene, far away across the continent from Cleveland. "Now wait a sec, wait a sec," he said. "What if we just, you know, muddle through?"

"What?"

"Just wait for him to get better."

"He won't."

"Okay, I'm not there, go ahead, whatever. But I hear people just recover, or they pass on."

"That's right. That's what happens."

"So maybe we should just, like I said, muddle through."

I said nothing. I wanted to do something. I wanted to

change things. I was impatient with this patience—angry. But perhaps it was the proper procedure after all. If you don't see the suffering, maybe you can see the proper procedure. Wait a sec.

My father was sitting by me as I made this call. He didn't stir. He was listening to something in his head; he was facing the flicker of the TV. When I hung up, he said, "Was that your brother?"

"I told him you're not feeling so well."

"That's a story-and-a-half, ain't it?" he asked.

My brother Bob came in, pulling off his tie. "Oh, what a day. I had to make six telephone calls. I couldn't get the guy on the phone. There are some things dad does, now I got to do them. Oh, boy. When's dinner? I got to have a shower. That was a day-and-a-half."

My brother Sid came in. "Is dad okay? Twenty minutes to dinner, isn't it? What's new?"

Our father turned from one son making sounds to another. "Are we having dinner?" he asked. "Let's have a little walk first, Herbert."

"That's a good idea."

"Just down the hall. Then we'll have dinner."

He was standing up, hands placed against the arms of the chair and then pressing. I waited for him. I kept thinking he should do these things by himself. Of course I'm like my mother. My job was to wait till he stood up. Okay. Now he was up and he turned halfway toward me. He wanted me to start the walk down the hall. "Try taking longer steps," I said.

"My eyes are blooey," my father said. "It's blur."

"I'll watch out for you."

"Don't feel safe. Help me."

"Try taking longer steps, dad. It's good exercise. You won't fall."

"Put your arm around me," he said. "Did I take my four-a-day pill? I have to take it every time I eat. Did I take it?"

"You took it, dad. You'll take it again after dinner."

"Let me tell you: seeing you again, even if my eyes are blooey, helps a lot. It's a help-and-a-half."

"Thank you, dad."

"And that Flossie's so good. I don't know without her. She helps so much. I don't know what I'd do."

"You keep her, dad."

"Mother thinks she costs too much. I'll tell you: she's jealous. Flossie likes me, I like her, so she's jealous. And I can't yell at her to shut up, I'm not strong enough."

"Just ride with it."

"I can't see, I can't hear, so she yells at me. I can't even go to sleep, she wakes me up. But that Flossie don't bother me." We stopped at the bathroom and he switched off the light. He turned it back on. "I want to talk with you soon, in case something happens to me, which it will."

He suddenly laughed aloud, and there was a silver flash at his mouth; and this speed recalled what was expert, powerful, and quick about my father when he used to wield the fruit hammer and run to the market in his truck and scream bloody murder at those who opposed him. The laugh disappeared. I heard his words in that narrow hallway: *In case something happens to me. Which it will.*

"Are you afraid, dad? Are you worried about something?"

"That's what everybody asks me. I don't think I'm worried."

"Is something on your mind?"

168

"I try not to worry. I don't want to lose Flossie. I try not to think about anything. My mind is a blank. Like my eyes—blooey. Only I have to walk now—" He began to tremble and he was pushing his fingers on my sleeve as if it were the arm of a chair. "I have to get up. I have to go for a walk now. Where's Flossie?"

"We're walking, dad."

These walks didn't last long. They were more like twitchings of the leg than walks. Sometimes he was silent, and then finished by saying, "Okay. I'll rest now." Sometimes he talked: "Oh yes, I used to be strong. I was very strong. I just don't want to do anything now. It's blooey and a blank. I don't care. Okay, I'll rest now."

We headed toward his room. I didn't like to walk in dark hallways. I wanted to go outside, although my legs twitched at the slowness of our procession. I felt like loping and roaming around him, but I walked with him and sometimes he asked to be steadied. He liked to touch. "Herbert, I want you to stay another day. Herbert, I have to talk to you."

"Dad, I was supposed to be home yesterday. My kids."

"One more day doesn't hurt. Didn't you tell me you're divorced? Stay one more day."

"What is it you want to talk about?"

A look of confused cunning on his face. "Too tired today. I'll tell you tomorrow. Put me to bed now."

"Dad, shouldn't you be doing something? That senior citizens bus, they would take you places—"

"A bunch of old people! And the smells! Nah," he said. "I try to have a hobby. When I get better, I'll go on a cruise. When I get better, I'll have a hobby. Stay to the day after tomorrow, Herbert. You got to make sure about Flossie. I got things to tell you when I'm a little rested."

Beneath the smells of sickness, the shallow breathing of

weakness, the shuffling steps and milky stare of age and retreat, there were questions which he could not put into words: who had he been, who was he now, was this the same person, why was he to suffer like this?

I think the rest of his family took these questions, in our different ways, as statements about the future for each of us.

Pain removes the suffering of the mind, being purely pain, the body seeking relief and the soul gladly surrendering. But he still insisted on his need, his rights. His soul had not surrendered. The time of brute clarity was not yet with him. His stubbornness stuttered and labored through his pain. He still had ideas about himself. He even had ideas about me. "Too bad about that wife of yours," he said. "Nice girl, smart, good behind she got on her. Whatever you did, you did it wrong."

"I know, dad. But it's complicated. I'd have preferred something else happened."

"Don't tell me. I can tell what you prefer."

"You always could, dad."

He sighed as if, being a father again, he had won some ease and victory. "Okay about the money, I'll sign the papers," he said, "if I can keep Flossie."

"Dad, I agree. That has nothing to do with it. You can keep Flossie if you sign or if you don't sign."

"Maybe I'll sign then."

"Dad, it's not a punishment. I think you want to do good with your money."

"You can't do good with it? I give to the synagogue, I give to the hospital, I give to Israel. How much can a man give? You can throw it out the window if you want to. My big kid—why you want me to give more?"

"Dad, if you don't do it, we can't. The government will take it."

"Can I keep Flossie?"

"Dad, I told you."

"I remember. Can I keep Flossie?"

"As far as I'm concerned, no matter what, yes."

"Can I keep Flossie?"

"Yes."

"Give me the papers. Give me a pen. Put my hand on the right place."

The next morning he woke up and rolled his body out of bed without help. He sat eating his cereal with a large spoon, silent and thinking, and suddenly said, "I think I'll go to my office today. I got a lot of work I haven't looked at."

He hadn't been to his office in almost a year. My brother and I helped him downstairs, through the gray and dim lights of glaucoma and cataracts, over the monstrous stairs and Parkinsonism, through the hazards of walking at the age of ninety. He seemed more alert than usual. He sat at his desk and opened the top drawer. He removed some papers—receipts, deposits, notices, contracts—now managed by an accountant. He used to be one of those prodigious human calculators who add up a column of figures at a glance. There was a new electronic calculator on the desk, and the old punch machines, too. He stared at the papers he was touching. After a few minutes, he looked up at my brother with a little smile. "I can't see," he said. He sat back in the chair and raised his arms a little, as if to stretch. He was smiling. "Well, I can afford to keep Flossie. I got enough resources."

"Of course you do, dad."

"Well, that's settled." He was still smiling. "We can all see that, can't we?"

171

"We sure can."

"You tell mother. You got to speak loud for me, son. You got to speak *loud*." He sat looking through the milky eyes and trying the edges of a sheet of paper with his thumb as if he were checking the sharpness of a knife. "Well, that's enough work for today. This wasn't Twelfth and Rockwell, was it? Take me back, please."

When we got home, Flossie was gone. Her spare uniform which hung in the broom closet was gone. Mother had given her an extra day's pay and told her to go. My father turned gray and sank to the couch. His mouth was working without words, but mother was no longer surprised by him, she knew all he had to say these days, and she had the answers: "I can give you your enema. I can wipe up when you piddle on the floor. You got to stand closer or sit down. I can wipe up."

"I don't want you to," he said. "And Flossie don't tell me about it, she just does it."

"I want that woman out of the house," my mother said. "Do you see how she touches him? Do you see how he grabs her?"

"She helps me down," he said. He turned to me. "Talk to mother. Plead with her. She won't listen to me. I want to keep Flossie. I need a nurse. I can afford her. Where's Flossie?"

"Mother," I said, "dad has earned it."

"She's making him like a baby." And she was closed, her head was closed down. "I've earned something, too," she said.

Nobody spoke. Flossie was gone, but she was still there. Flossie was still there, but she was gone.

"Herbert, let's go for a ride," my father said. "I'm not hungry. I'm dizzy. I can sleep if you give me a ride."

172

My mother stared at me now with a strange quiet curiosity. It was the look of a brave person observing an ominous stranger, and waiting. I think she expected rage and biting. She was ready. She was wrong. Yet perhaps giving way to her will was the most correct procedure of the several incorrect choices at this time in our lives. She needed to hold things together, put bacon fat in the eggs, open the letters. It was the same strength that smashed the steaming flesh of a rabid dog. The continuity of possession of her husband kept her blood hot and high. Furiously she fought to possess what could not be possessed. Life for her meant serving in the way she had learned, by whatever procedures history had taught her, even if this also meant giving an enema to the husband who still felt shame.

I said she was staring at me. I was staring at her. Her secret self, ferocious and tired, unyielding and helpless, stricken with the loneliness Hilda had promised her long ago, gazed back at me from the depths. I thought I saw the smile of Hilda and Anna, the family smile, Frieda's smile, bestir the corners of her mouth. In another blink it might have seemed triumphant—the smile of ridding herself of Flossie. But it was hopeless in its victory.

"Are we going, Herbert?" my father asked. "Help me."

He was satiated with loss. Grief closed him down, too.

"Should I ride with you?" mother asked.

"*No!*" I shouted, and both my father and my mother were startled.

"Quiet, shush, I'm not the deaf one," she said. "I was just being polite. I got better things to do with my time. And you think I don't have things to do for your father I don't even like to mention?"

She would watch by her man till the end. At the end

things should be sweeter. In his own time of need, he deserved better. This lady was still the wife he chose.

"What you need to ride for?" mother asked us. "I'll take you for a walk, Sam. At least that's a little exercise."

"Herbert, take me for a ride."

"Mother. We'll be back later. Dad needs a ride."

"You just came in," she said. She looked at me and put her hands up. "Okay! Okay! Don't throw fire from your face like that! You and your father and your grandfather, all the men in this family, they always do just what they want!"

What my father wanted just now: he didn't want to be home on a Monday, Wednesday, or Friday without Flossie, or on another day when he would only be waiting for her to help him down.

When I returned to San Francisco, one of my sons had a cold and a cough, and he was blurred by fever and antibiotics, and he lay propped against a pillow with eyes vague and mouth slack and a froglike blinking expression, suddenly like the very old man he will be in eighty years or so, if he lives that long, and like me in forty, when I too will have forgotten where Twelfth and Rockwell was in Cleveland, Ohio.

At last the mind lays by its troubles and relents. At last the mind relents and lets the body have its way.

11 HIS FIRSTBORN daughter has given her-self, her husband, his parents, her parents, a child—his firstborn grandchild. Some babies are Saturday night spe-cials, projected out of a bump in the dark; others are sched-uled as the software of history, the thing that's now to be done in order to extend memory, input procedures for output programming. This child was sought by everyone up and down the line, a convergence of desire. Fortunately it still happened like that. She was not the opposite of what she was. As she struggled for the nipple, bawled for her pleasure and fright in the world, her grandfather watched and thought: like everyone else around here, she'll do what she wants. That's what she is. As the cohorts advance, we are surpassed and had better be blessed about it.

He gave his mother the news on the long distance telephone: "You're a great-grandmother. I didn't wait for the evening rates."

"Oh dear, oh dear, oh dear."

"It's a girl."

"Oh dear—you're sure?"

"Will you tell dad? Make him hear?"

As she found breath, he answered the questions about name, weight, health, religious affiliation of hospital, exact hour, ethnic connection of attending physician, zip codes of Congregationalist relatives, and how he, her son, the newborn grandfather, happened to feel when he first noticed what had occurred. "Fine, fine," he said. "She looks like you, mother"—this slick steaming orange cheek-puffing little lizardlike slither of greediness.

"Oh, sha. Don't be funny. I bet she's pretty."

"She is, mother." He was remembering a sepia photograph of softness and sweetness, his mother as a child. "Tell dad the line continues," he said.

"Your father will be glad. He's awake. I hear him in the hall. He stands and looks out the window, but he can't see anything. I'll tell him. Don't nag, I'll tell him."

Since it was her first great-grandchild, she forgave him for not waiting to call until after six. Temporarily she adopted the formal diction and dignity suitable for a great-grandmother. This was optional, not required, until real life intervened and she could be done with ceremony.

"He knows already. I think he can tell. Your father is bothering me already I should explain what's happening."

He remembered the mother who assured him love exists, a person can marry again; love exists, a person treasures his children; love exists because the line continues and life is never done. The great-grandmother still woke and sought out her privacy at dawn, cooking, doing the laundry with generic brand bleach and detergent in industrial-size boxes, baking oatmeal raisin cookies for middle-aged sons and a husband who couldn't see them, mailing preserves in shoe boxes and premiums from the Premium Room to family around the country, still dreaming of her doom of love and seeking ways to name it.

Despite her concentration on evening rates, generic brands, and the Premium Room, she was extravagant in her expectations. She did not give up.

The child lurched to suckle a few minutes after her birth.

And this other mother, who once was his daughter, who had held his hand down the Bourdon road to Petionville in Haiti, naming the things as he named them, learning the flowers and the words for them, the difference between a mule and a donkey, a horse and a pony, a lizard and a joke; and later insisted that a family belongs together, even if it's not; and later planted her winter garden at Kibbutz Gan Shmuel, the Garden of Samuel, as a war began and she told him she was frightened. Now she was what she always promised to become, daughter and mother in her turn.

12 "HE WONDERS why you don't come to see him when you have a grandchild," my brother said. "He feels left out. He says *he* was the grandfather, so if you are now, what is he?"

"Is that what he thinks?"

"He's lonely, Herb."

Dad talked with Sid in the white light of the kitchen at midnight, seeming during that quiet hour to understand and hear, puzzling aloud and asking for answers. There were no longer very good ones. He asked the questions again and again. He stopped to tilt his head and listen. He asked the questions again.

When I came to visit I felt once more like the boy who had run away, had gone to New York to school, had returned to Cleveland from other cities with wives and young children, dropped by on his ticket from Africa or Haiti or Russia or Israel, had been making this trip with dufflebag over his shoulder for many years. Grandfatherliness fell away on a familiar journey.

"Hi, dad."

"Is it you?"

"Hello, dad! No, mother, I'm not starving, but I guess I can eat—"

It began once more with a meal. It was usually dinnertime in Cleveland, except when it was lunchtime. My father sat perched on the edge of his chair as mother put food on his plate. He stared straight ahead. His lips were gray. Sid cut meat for him and put a spoon in his hand. The fingers curled slowly about the spoon and the spoon explored for the morsels. He was silent, but I believed he would speak to me before long. He was getting used to my presence. The cautious attention on his face, which sometimes seemed like abstraction and distance, meant he was getting used to the new resonances in his Arctic isolation. His journey seemed to be ever further north.

In the familiar way, mother worried that I might have eaten on the flight from San Francisco, thereby subverting my appetite. At home there are changes and there is the lack of change. She had prepared some questions for me out of her lifelong studies in the field of nourishment of everybody in general and of me in particular. These questions arose naturally, and were modern versions of the ones she asked forty years ago, more, when Tom Moss shared a peanut butter and jelly Wonder Bread sandwich with me, that sticky stuff you can transform into silly putty and hurl at enemies or girls; he got oatmeal cookies in return. This was her tireless fruit Jell-O mold research, her patty melt investigation. America had a continuing frontier in the terra incognita of peristalsis. "At least is it quality junk food," she asked, "I learned that word, that junk food you eat all the time? Is it balanced vitamins-added junk food you're ruining your stomach? I would only like to know where it comes from, some central headquarters junk food factory? They say it's fast food, I don't think it's so fast, unless they're talking about how it goes through you, but I bet it goes through you slow. Is it health natural quality junk fast food at least, that organism stuff full of bugs? And I heard about that pizza, you take the bones out first when you cook it? In my day the Eyetalians ate spaghetti, they even made spaghetti, ravioli, on a picnic out at Huntington Park, not all those funny fishes people cook now, put the heartburn down there. Pizza pies, it's heavy. A person can get diverticulis like I got, she can't eat those heavy pies. So in your city, you eat egg omelets with fresh cottage cheese and fruit in it, like I read and saw with my own eyes? Otherwise I wouldn't believe."

"Dad!" I said. "Your great-granddaughter asked about you."

"He can't hear you," mother said. "She's only two months old. He doesn't get jokes."

He didn't even say, *what?*

"She can't talk yet, can she?" my mother asked. "In our family some of us are early talkers. I bet she's an early talker."

"He can't hear when there's background noise," Sid explained. "He can't hear when—"

"In a month or so, you'll see, she'll be counting to ten,

180

she'll read the license plates on the street, get a little sun in the stroller, she'll be asking about her great-grandmother."

"—he can't hear," Sid said, "when there are several people talking. Maybe he hears sometimes, but he doesn't pay attention. He turns off."

"I can turn off too," mother said. "Anytime I want to, I can turn off. But then how would you like it?"

"Dad!" I said.

"Can she really talk?" mother asked. "At her age, it would be a miracle, but take it from me, miracles happen."

"Dad!" I said. "Your great-granddaughter is two months old already!"

"It's no use," mother said. "Don't make an excitement."

"He gets nervous if you insist," Sid said. "He gets sick if he can't understand."

"Tell him I'll talk with him later," I said to my brother.

"I think he knows that. He can wait. Plenty of time."

"Nothing but," mother said. "Not going to a park, not playing rummy, just thinks about not feeling good. Sometimes I think he dreams about the schwartzeh, Flossie. A cruise! You know that's all he does now is wait?"

I stood with her in the kitchen, helping in the drying of dishes, while she slammed the silverware into the drawer. Angrily she jangled it in a towel first. She did not leave it to rinse in the metal grill available for slow drying purposes when her emotion was less high. "I wish you wouldn't talk about dad like that when he's sitting there," I said.

"He doesn't hear."

"He knows," I said.

"You don't have to live with him. You don't have to put up with this. He couldn't even go to Anna's funeral—too blooey, he said. So you can come to town and be Mister-Nice-Guy."

"Let's talk about something else, mother. The kids are fine. The great-granddaughter is fine. There are lots of nice things. What else you want to talk about?"

"Chanukah," she said. It was the first day of my visit and she wanted to exercise no personal grudges. "I been thinking. Let's talk about the goyim and Chanukah."

My brother walked dad down the hall to his bathroom, where mother had spread newspapers on the floor, and I sat with her at the kitchen table to attend to her view about Chanukah. Two of the things that helped her get over things were theories and judgments. She had a rich stock of them; as she had a Premium Room, she seemed to have a Conclusion Room. "The way I see it, they took Chanukah from us and called it Christmas or Yule or Nole, couldn't make up their mind, Rudolph the Red Reindeer, Santy Claus, Snow White, so many other angels who could count? The trees are pretty, I'll give them that, but I wouldn't want one in my house—sheds on the carpet. So then they took Pesach and called it Easter. Yom Kippur, what? Veterans Day? A little early, and too sad for them. Seems like it's all on permanent loan. Okay, so I got my own back. I'm taking Halloween right now. I'm not a philosopher, I don't just talk for nothing like some people you know who"—I knew who—"I'm doing it. I haven't decided what I'll use Halloween for, how should I know, not studying the literal arts in the Ivory League. But it's got to be good for something better'n funny faces and sick kids from too much colored sugar."

"I don't eat it anymore, just the candy corns, I like those," I admitted.

"When you're say over fifty, time you stopped eating the corns, too. Have a little dignity, please. Naturally, I admit it's nice to eat candy corn and you don't take dope, *do you?* like some other young fathers—"

"Grandfathers," I said.

"All right, already. Trouble is, we don't need a holiday just that month of the year. Maybe I'll save it for an emergency—one more time Israel has to teach the Arabs a lesson. I can't do it all by myself with bonds."

"Why didn't dad want to change the world?" I asked her, trying to slip sideways through the maze of welcoming rumination.

She fell silent. The question reminded her of something. She shook her head. She did not want to be drawn into sadness just now. But she would answer this question. "He used to. Now he got small things on his mind. He thinks about his medicine. He has nightmares so I can't sleep—I use your room—I have to sleep in your room—you don't mind your mother sleeping in your room, do you?"

It hadn't been my room for thirty-five years.

"I can't sleep anyways, so naturally—why when he can't sleep, what the devil he's thinking, I want to sleep? He groans, he makes noises, fights like the old days. Talks in his dreams but he won't talk to me. He's what you shouldn't even call awake, I can hardly get a word in all day, just *Frieda, Frieda, I don't feel so good.* And then when I can't, sometimes he sleeps so quiet it scares me. Like dead. It scares me, Herbert. So when it's too early to make noise, wake everybody up, huzzaballoo-balloo, I find time to think. Not that I'd tell you. I think about things." She peeked shrewdly at me, waited for me to ask, but then shrugged her shoulders. "Not that I remember anyway." Her face was flushed, her wrists red and raw, too, the milky skin and unwrinkled brow suddenly burning. She hid her hands, those blushing hands. It embarrassed her to confess that she did some considering of matters at dawn. Was she planning to tell me again she had another husband, another lover? "From time to time, I wouldn't want to do it too much—in the dark, I'm alone, I'm all by myself, it's usual, it's nothing unusual these days . . . *I think.*"

"About what?"

"I loved him the best I could! I think, Herbert!"

I looked away from the flushed face, elsewhere, anywhere. The open pantry. The marching cans of utility soup. Even a son should have mercy on his mother. I gave her a chance to hide herself with more words, but she had nothing but silence to add. She got up and shut the pantry so the soup would stay fresh and cool. I waited, cleared my throat (phlegm? she would ask, some hot water with lemon?), and said, "What does dad do in the dark?"

"Not what he used to do."

She didn't want to talk about him anymore. She had said too much. She wanted to talk, but she didn't want me to ask questions which crowded the kitchen with reproach. I had no right to take aim at her. She wasn't sure I had fully taken in the dire report about herself—*thinking.*

"Your brother put up a bed for you in the library," she said.

I slept under the painting my father and mother bought when they were visiting their first grandchildren in Haiti twenty-five years ago. There were card-players; a good kind of painting for my father. Mother liked it because there was a lot of color, goes well in a library, otherwise you just got all those brown books, no color, no life, maybe a few plants. They had decided on this painting by a young man who was now a sick old one and had stopped painting. Mother noticed that the nice colored in Haiti were well-educated, intelligent, friendly, spoke French if that's what it was they were speaking. Dad asked if they had any real estate worthy of the name in this place—bricks, basements, foundations, *real* real estate, office-warehouse deals, really real property. He didn't notice any, a bunch of shacks, no developments or nice subdivisions.

Under the painting by Wilson Bigaud I walked once again down the Petionville road with my eldest daughter. It was a memory of sweetness which had become a talisman. I stretched, remembered goats, flowers, lizards, my firstborn child, and slept. In the dark of my parents' house in Cleveland, now and here, for the first time in months, I dreamed of my former wife. We were standing in the house we had shared in San Francisco, she was talking with me as we used to speak, it was familiar and domestic. But then a stranger appeared. The man with whom she lives hurried by, heading toward the kitchen with a basket of trash for the back stairway, nodding hello to me, wearing only the blue boxer shorts my father wears. My wife, former wife, hastened to join him, leaving me wondering why I was in a strange house. She ran trippingly and girlishly toward the kitchen, slightly pigeon-toed, as is our daughter. The man she ran toward is large, quiet, and polite. She ran gawkily and girlishly after him. I stood in the empty room.

I woke. It was cold in Cleveland. There were noises from the kitchen and noises from the laundry room. Like the great strategists of history, Napoleon and Alexander, mother could be in two places at once, deploying her resources with the help of modern technology, banks of buttons, oven timers. She wakes before dawn, dreaming of sheets, shirts, socks to darn (even if they're cheap to buy, that doesn't mean there's a law against mending), breakfast for the visitor (I had developed poached egg and granola convictions), while my own dreams did no good work at all. It's a relief to foretell, have a cup of Postum, and fulfill. When I followed the thumping and stirring noises, my thoughts gloomy and infected, hers cheerful, she began a course of canny propaganda with the goal of getting a decent meal to wend its way down my throat, start the day right, calcium for growing bones; plus toast, muffins, her own blueberry ones, revised in her laboratory from the recipe on the box, her *own* recipe because she added extra strictly fresh-frozen blueberries from the famed blueberry bogs of Birds Eye. Happy food for a growing grandfather.

She wanted to talk. As sometimes happens in lonesome love, I was unaware of how much I wanted to talk. "Morning, morning,"—a dawn grouch and growl which my wives didn't hear from me anymore. It was dad's voice I was offering her for old time's sake.

We took breakfast together in the whitening winter light as the first commuter traffic from Shaker Heights began downshifting on the hill outside. Stray December snowflakes beat in gusts at the window. The glass was rattling, storm predicted, airport closing, so mother suggested I put on a pair of warm socks. She thought she might have some of my old khaki ones put away in the Shredded Ralston closet for just this sort of emergency. It's troubling for the digestion to eat breakfast with tense, chilled toes crisped on the rungs of the chair. My time of khaki socks was a generation ago, is she organizing a World War Two Surplus Museum? I thought. But I kept the peace; so did she, unused to dawn conversation.

Kitchen deployments filled the silence. Future nutrition spoke for us. She was paring potatoes, washing greens, organizing provisions. When I turned to look at Fairhill Road outside—wind, snowflakes, headlights—she slipped a dab of peach jam onto my blueberry muffin, since I wasn't looking anyway and it's wasteful not to enjoy something she had canned last September in my favorite Mason jar. Wasn't peach my favorite? So why discuss? She threw a fast challenge across the table. I said nothing, although I was now biting into a peach thumbprint.

In this low-tech garden of carrot greens and parsley, beets and potato slices thumping into a pot—soup for lunch is prepared while first breakfast is consumed—the pipes under the sink curled and rumbled like snakes whose heads and tails were busy elsewhere. Who ever could complain when a slash of peach jam appears like a miracle from no-place, free of any extra charge? Certainly not a son who doesn't need a quarrel on this morning of his life. Mother sighted a tuber from the Farmers' Market along the curli-cue edges of a paring knife, squinted, and got ready for one of my favorite dishes—uncanned soup. What she was mak-ing was always, on that day, one of my favorite dishes; history shows this. As yet I couldn't determine what all my favorite dishes would turn out to be that coming noontime.

She wanted not to wake the others. She said very softly, "You have enough? You finished already? You hungry?"

"That's good. Thanks, mother."

"With all the reading you say you do, you notice how our modern breakfast of today is still the most important meal, bar none?"

Right. Of the five or six meals a day, including major snacks and stomach-soothers, the one we were eating at present was the one which determined character and desti-ny. Else why would we be wasting our time here eating it? A family marches on its stomach; if not, the belly rumbles; weakness, anemia, and calcium deficiency ensue by 11 A.M.; disaster at the noon whistle. Her imagination of nourish-ment was passionate, like the imagination of love; faithful and fond, like few loves. Actually, when you came right down to it, the home-canned peach preserves went pretty well with the Birds Eye fresh-frozen blueberry muffins.

A scraping noise in the hall. Slippers. Silently stalking no prey with his tiny steps, my father appeared. He was chilled; his face was blue. The eyes stared. His hands touched the smeared darker places on the walls where his hands had touched them before, guiding himself through the dimmed universe. He was wearing blue boxer shorts, which surprised me, although he always wore blue boxer shorts—they were the blue shorts of the polite large man in the dream. My father grasped a bottle of his morning medicine in his hand along with a spoon. He wanted help in pouring. I read the label and filled the tablespoon and he sucked in a chalky liquid. I'm not sure he noticed who had taken the bottle from his hand, tilted it, fed him the medicine. "Good morning, dad!" I shouted.

"What's that? What do you want?"

"He doesn't put his aid on. Sometimes he wants me to clean it with Q-tips. That Flossie did it for him, spoiled him. He could do it himself with a toothpick. I think he doesn't want to hear."

He looked at her and said, "It don't help."

"It's Herb," I said, "should I get your hearing aid?"

"I know who it is," he said. "Didn't you just say good morning and ask me something?"

"Good morning, dad!"

"Is there anything to eat? Something hot. I'm shivering."

"Dad, I'm getting your robe. You shouldn't walk around like that."

"I need something hot right away. Don't feel so good— my morning blooey feeling I got."

"Sit down, sit down, so sit down already," mother said as I helped him into the bathrobe, guiding his arms.

"Did you have breakfast already? You didn't wait?"

"How can he wait for you? How do I know when you might get up? Half the time you go to the bathroom, I put your breakfast out, and then you go right back to bed and I never see you. And sometimes maybe not, so how can I make plans for a meal? How many feedings can a person do around here?"

"Dad, I'm having breakfast. I want another cup of coffee with you, dad."

"For me just Postum. Can't take my morning nap if I drink too much coffee."

"So stay up, dad. You can sleep later."

"What? What? Going out later? You just got here."

As I shouted at my father he stared straight ahead; he emitted his answers. Mother stood there with the table-spoon and his medicine, watching us both, her two crazies. I looked at the spoon and then at the cross-hatchings and maze of her fingertips. She saw me staring and touched my cheek. "Not just him, I'm getting there also," she said. "Are my fingers too rough for you?"

Her voice was low, as if this question were a secret between us.

Say something nice, I thought. I said, "Nice fingers, mother. You still keep them busy."

"Maybe too much," she said. "Trouble is, even too much is never enough."

"What what what?" A deaf bark from my father.

"Even last year he would ask me, *Too much what, Frieda?* He got mad or mean and that was a lot better—*too much what?* He would say all that. It's a tragedy. When I lost my mother, okay, I was a girl, I had the chance to have other

189

friends, I had my sister. But Anna was my big sister. Gone. And my husband—not gone, so sometimes it's worse. Do I know why? Can you tell me where it all stops? Even a graduate from the Ivory League I bet you can't."

My youngest brother, Bob, the baby of the family, a bald middle-aged man, looked in and asked, "What's all the commotion? My alarm didn't even go off yet. It's too early for commotion."

Mother waited for me to accept her challenge. Where does it all stop? I couldn't answer. Unlike my father, she was not a gambling person, she preferred sure things, there were too many unsure things already without her adding to them, but she won the bet. I didn't answer.

When she opened my mail, listened in on my bowels, picked up the extension phone to study my conversational skills, explored my pockets, wallet, or notebooks for clues, or simply backed me up against the refrigerator and grilled me like a station house sergeant, her method followed from an assumption—love is always asking, deciphering plus *asking*. I did not share this assumption. What American men seek from women is engrossed acceptance, not this interrogation, not her need to make me testify, not totalitarian love! An occasional lack of interest helps, too. American women have something else on their minds besides husbands, sons, and lovers, thank the newborn genderless God. But finally I needed to learn that this other way was my mother's love, it was what Hilda and Anna brought through the dangerous mountain-high waves of the Atlantic, shattered ice like bits of glass rushing down the heaving water; it is a kind of love, and I could cleave to my American desires but I had better also accept her terms. It was what she was serving. It would also be totalitarian to demand what I happened to like from someone who was serving something different. Late in all our lives I could eat her idea of food, wear darned socks (maybe limp a little), tell her a soothing embarrassing personal secret now and then, give her something to ruminate upon. Why should any woman offer just what *I* happened to prefer? Once I accepted this— she had her own right to the madness of love, as I have mine—I learned to enjoy her cooking and sewing. The oatmeal was good, the *poached* eggs; the springiness of bunched yarn in a sock reminded me of a long and honorable frugality.

It was as lonely as Hilda had predicted it would be. Frieda remembered love, but memory slips away. What remains is the haunting—the desiring edges of memory, the moments of pain and thrill and the dream images of the past. Now her husband stood at the window, counting the stars he could no longer see. Sometimes in the past he had wakened for the task of star-counting, and she had interrupted her predawn baking and cleaning to join him there, by the morning light which flooded over them before they were finished. This haunted lady kept Hilda and Anna alive, and called my father back to life, and reminded her sons of what they too would miss, lack, lose, because everyone loses it, misses it, perhaps finds it and then it slips away. The blessings of day after day. The blessings of the moment, possession of the time, a continual refreshment in appetite. For the sake of these moments we make deals with the impenetrability and strangeness, man to woman, husband to wife, son to mother, which wakes us to do the laundry and the sitting in the middle of the night. Nobody counted the stars and waited for her anymore. Ferociously she held to her haunted greed, and passed it on to me.

My good fortune was undeserved. Our family lived long; it seemed to be a genetic defect. I came to knowledge in time, as her breath grew short up hills and the number of her breaths came no longer to seem infinite. She tried to control everything, but matters of mortality lay beyond her insistence. She knew the essential pains reached deeper than her kitchen skills, her household management, and yet she never stopped trying. She told my father to shape up at ninety-two. She wasn't letting him dream of any Caribbean cruise with any Flossie. She advised me to do things differently although I had seldom taken her advice in the past. Steadily she emitted her good counsel as it happened to occur to her. No wonder she was bravely and eternally at odds with language and men!

The glitter and edge of the words she used, even the errors with which she sought to find her truths, were part of her effort to close the distance between the love she expressed and the love she intended, the predawn silence between the loneliness she felt and gave and the loneliness she tried not to tell and tried to relieve. Again and again she discovered how words were no good, not good enough, and therefore God in his waste and wisdom gives us life also, plus more words, plus clear intentions we know only in the sharpest moments of hope and loss. He scatters light everywhere; he spills darkness around it.

She looked at my father, frozen and silent in his chair, and said suddenly: "His Name That Sat on Him was Death."

"What's that, mother?"

"Something I read in the paper this morning."

"You read that in the newspaper?"

She flushed and fidgeted. She was deeply embarrassed. "Don't ask so many questions. I read that in the Book."